DOGCATCHER IN THE RYE

ELLEN RIGGS

Dogcatcher In the Rye

Copyright © 2020 Ellen Riggs

ISBN 978-1-989303-49-8 eBook
ISBN 978-1-989303-48-1 Book
ASIN B0859NGJQM Kindle
ASIN TBD Paperback

Publisher: Ellen Riggs
www.ellenriggs.com
Cover designer: Lou Harper
Editor: Serena Clarke
20032 11541

CHAPTER ONE

K eats ran to the front window and stood on his hind legs to look out at the driveway. He didn't even lean on the wall, just stood upright like a circus dog. I'd taught him plenty of tricks, but that one he knew before we met a few months ago. He could turn a full circle in a few quick hops and never lost his balance. The slim, shaggy black-and-white dog with one blue eye and one brown was living proof of why border collies top the list on the canine intelligence scale.

"Who is it, buddy?" I asked. "Tell me it's not another casserole delivery."

He directed his blue eye at me, and I could have sworn it rolled. Keats had the most expressive face I'd ever seen on a dog. I was getting better at figuring out what he was thinking. And he was *always* thinking. Some days I was convinced he was smarter than me, if only because my brain hadn't fully recovered since the incident that had brought us together.

"Help me keep this short, okay?" I said, smoothing

my hair. I wished I'd put on makeup earlier. When I lived in the city, there was no way I'd even think of opening the door without mascara, eyeliner and earrings. "Create a diversion if you need to. We've got a ton of errands in town."

Keats' tail wagged once, twice, then drifted down. It didn't look promising. With all the visitors we'd had since moving to the farm a week earlier, I'd barely been able to get anything done. The old tradition of stopping by with a warm welcome was alive and well in Clover Grove. It was sweet, but time consuming. Keats had no patience for it at all. He was a dog who liked to be doing, not sitting around making small talk.

No one arrived empty handed. The cupboards that had been pretty much bare now held jam in five flavors and preserves both sweet and sour. The fridge and freezer were full of pies, cakes and heartier dishes. Mostly, there were eggs—dozens of them in shapes, sizes and colors I never knew existed. Meanwhile, there were about 40 generous hens in my own coop, producing more eggs than I could use, at least until my inn opened next month. Hopefully my guests would love omelets.

When I left Clover Grove for college 15 years ago, the town had been moving away from its agricultural roots. The homesteading trend was bringing people back to the land in droves. I had mocked that trend once, but now I was basically doing the same. Things had a way of biting you in the butt in farm country.

I opened the door at the precise moment someone gave a firm knock. It startled me and maybe that's why I gasped even before I saw Lloyd Boyce standing on the porch in a uniform. I hadn't seen Lloyd since high school, and I hoped time had been kinder to me than it had been to him. His ginger hair had not so much silvered as faded to a dull tan and his freckled face was lined and haggard. Still, his eyes were a striking blue and he held himself as if he knew how to use his charm if he felt like it.

"Well, hello Lloyd," I said. "How nice to see you. You haven't changed a bit."

It was the kind of polite lie you learned to tell early in Clover Grove and I'd never outgrown the habit. My former colleagues had teased me about it, but it hadn't slowed my climb up the corporate ranks.

"Hi Ivy," Lloyd said. "You look great, too."

I could tell from the slight twitch of his lips that he probably meant it. In high school, he'd run in the same circles as Asher, my older brother. Lloyd had always given me the creeps but I must have hidden it well because he invited me to his senior prom. Ash was outraged—the invitation defied "bro code"—but I'd declined anyway. My tenth grade social life wasn't exactly thriving but there was no way I was dating Lloyd Boyce.

Maybe Lloyd remembered that old rejection, too, because his eyes dropped to his black work boots, which looked freshly polished. His black uniform with the town crest was crisp and fit well. The belt around his waist had a holster over his left hip that held what appeared to be a can of pepper spray. A short baton balanced that out on his right hip, and another device hung further back. The weapons made me even more uneasy.

"What can I do for you, today, Lloyd? I don't see a pie

or preserves, so I'm assuming it's not a housewarming visit."

"Right. I'm here on business." Lloyd pressed his thin lips together and peered over my shoulder. "There's been a complaint."

"A complaint? Already? I've only been here a week. I haven't had time to get into trouble." I had a good poker face after more than a decade of work in human resources and I was grateful for it now. "I mean, other than eating too much pie. Could I interest you in a slice? I've got apple, blueberry and pecan. You really can't go wrong with any of them."

"I don't eat pie on duty," Lloyd said, rising on the toes of his boots to look over my other shoulder.

"Let me get you a glass of water then. Or a cup of coffee." I scanned the gravel driveway, expecting to see cars arriving with nosy neighbors. It wouldn't be long till the Clover Grove rumor mill started churning about Lloyd's visit. If it wasn't already.

His eyes came back to land on me. "Where is he?"

"Where is who? I'm on my own here till my first paying guests arrive."

That caught his attention. "Guests?"

"Clients. Customers. Maybe you've heard that I'm opening a small inn. Coming from Boston, I know how eager people are to enjoy the farm experience."

"This isn't a farm." He shook his head in apparent disgust. "It's a petting zoo."

"Hobby farm, then. Would you like to come down to the barn and meet the alpaca? It's a beautiful day for a stroll."

September was my favorite month in Clover Grove. The worst of the heat had lifted, but it was still balmy. My goal was to open before the fall colors came in. The surrounding hills had some of the best views in the country.

"I get enough walking in my job," Lloyd said. "And I don't have any interest in your misfits."

"Misfits! That's a terrible thing to say. The rescued animals here are all very sweet." Except for the pig, who was intent on killing me, but no need to mention that. As an Animal Services field agent, Lloyd might take issue.

"The County doesn't endorse this farm, Ivy. I hope you know that. It's been nothing but trouble, especially after that heiress took over and started her stupid online show. It attracted swarms of idiots."

"I have full confidence that the County will enjoy the tourist dollars my guests bring. I think my inn's going to be a big hit. People will love frolicking with the goats, milking the cows and seeing lambs being born. They'll eat five-star meals and go home feeling restored."

"Sounds like a commercial," he said, taking a step back.

I pressed my lips together to stop more words from tumbling out. My nerves were showing. Initially, I'd been on the fence about coming home to Clover Grove, but the former owner, Hannah Pemberton, had tracked me down in Boston and asked me to buy Runaway Farm. *Insisted*, actually. It was the strangest thing I'd ever experienced, other than the incident that prompted the offer—an incident I was desperate to forget. I couldn't help but think the universe was pulling me home. Now that I was back here, I had moments of wishing the universe had sent me someplace else. When forces like that align, however, who are we to argue?

"What happened with Hannah isn't my business," I said. The online show he despised, The Princess and the Pig, was hilarious and provocative. I was watching old episodes to educate myself about Runaway Farm and its makeover into an inn. "But I assure you I'm serious about this inn and the community. I have to be."

Lloyd shook his head and frowned. "City slickers."

I wasn't sure whether he was insulting me or my future guests, so I let it slide. "Eventually all chickens come home to roost, I guess."

His eyes lit up and I mentally cursed myself for giving him the opening he wanted.

"Speaking of chickens," he said. "Edna Evans called Animal Services today saying your dog attacked her hens."

Keats chose that exact moment to stick his head between my knees and stare up at Lloyd. Then he gave a sharp woof. The dog had told me off often enough that I knew it was a reproof.

"Those chickens were on my property," I said. "Keats simply rounded them up and took them home. Not a single feather was ruffled."

"Edna said they came rushing onto her porch clucking like the devil himself was after them."

Keats *had* been a trifle overeager. He had more experience herding sheep and the hens' vertical moves added complexity to the maneuver. Still, all the hens had arrived safely.

"That's quite an exaggeration, Lloyd. Keats is a herding dog. I've been working with him for months."

"Herding? In the city?" He gave me a skeptical look.

"All over the state, actually. Would you like to see his certificates? He's a prizewinner."

Keats gave a high-pitched whine, as if my bragging were beneath him. It was beneath both of us, since we'd only passed beginner level. He was a natural, but we were just getting started.

Lloyd shook his head. "Doesn't matter. Your dog was chasing livestock and that's not tolerated here. The consequences start with a fine and end with—"

I tensed, squeezing my shins together. Keats made a strangled sound and pulled back. "I hope you're not threatening my dog, Lloyd. Keats is the best dog on earth. I moved back here to give him a better life."

"You moved back because some heiress gave you a sweet deal on this place. How'd you manage that, anyway?"

I glanced around, feeling almost embarrassed at my good fortune. The big old red brick farmhouse had been renovated beautifully, keeping the best features of the original and adding luxurious finishes. There was a new wing at the back with spacious bedrooms and spa-like bathrooms for the guests. I still felt like I was living in a boutique hotel, but it would become home soon enough. My sister, Daisy, was helping me add the final touches.

"Just lucky, I guess," I said. "Hannah saw an article about me saving Keats from a dangerous criminal, and thought I needed a break."

"I save dogs every day and no one gives me breaks like that."

His face twitched into a frown and for a second I felt sorry for him. "You've done well for yourself, Lloyd, at least from what Ash tells me."

"What'd your brother say?" Now he sounded worried.

I bit my lower lip. Asher was an officer with Wolff County's police department. Sometimes he shared confidential things because I was out of town and couldn't get him in trouble with gossip. Now that I lived here, I'd have to be more careful, especially since my memory wasn't always my friend these days.

"Something about a girl...?" I began. "You got married?"

"I got divorced," he said. "Well, almost."

"Oh. I'm sorry, Lloyd. That must have been hard."

He waved away my pity. "I've found someone new. You probably remember Mandy McCain."

"The baker, of course. Her grandmother runs Clover Grove Country Store. I've loved that place forever."

"The store's outdated now, but the land's worth a bomb with the way the town's developing. Mandy should sell while she can and get out." His frown lines deepened. "This place isn't what you remember, Ivy."

"I bet Clover Grove still has a big heart, just like when we were growing up."

He gave a little smirk as he pulled a device from his equipment belt. "I'll show some heart today by letting you off with the minimum fine. As a homecoming present."

I gasped. "A fine! Lloyd, you can't fine me for escorting someone's hens from my property to their own home. That's ridiculous."

"You're not in Boston anymore, Ivy. We take animal welfare seriously here."

Heat whooshed up from my belly and blew out my diplomacy circuits. "You're a dogcatcher. You round up strays so the County can euthanize them. How is that taking animal welfare seriously?"

Color rose under Lloyd's tan, swamping his freckles. "I'm just following the rules. Your dog was chasing livestock. End of story."

"Oh, it's not the end of this story. I'm going to contest this fine. What are my rights?"

Lloyd shrugged. "You have the right to pay the fine now or pay double if you're late."

Keats whined, as if to warn me, and I took a deep breath. I didn't lose my temper often, but when I did... well, the last time landed me on the news, in the hospital, and ultimately out of a job. Losing it again now certainly wouldn't help my farm-themed inn. I didn't want a blot on my record with Animal Services.

Maybe it wasn't too late to turn things around. I took another deep breath and closed my eyes. Normally my best friend, Jilly Blackwood, would step in when I lost my tact, but she wouldn't be here to visit for another few weeks. I'd just have to channel my inner executive—the one who'd hired and fired hundreds of people for a large corporation.

"Lloyd, I'm sorry about my tone. I'm just so anxious about all of this." I gestured from the big red barn to the paddock, where two Holstein heifers leaned over the fence watching us. "There's so much riding on the launch of my inn. Obviously I don't want to get off on the wrong foot with Animal Services."

Lloyd didn't even look up from his device. His big fingers moved with surprising speed, until he punched a button with his thumb. A bright orange ticket spit out the bottom, like a neon tongue. The whirring noise it made covered the sound of Keats's low grumble... or so I hoped. I snapped my fingers and the dog subsided.

"I heard that." Lloyd tore off the ticket with a flourish. "He growled."

"He did not growl. He makes mumbling sounds all the time. That's all."

"I'm in animal control. I know an aggressive dog when I hear it."

"Aggressive! Are you kidding me? He's a border collie. He herds sheep and does agility. He dances on his hind legs while balancing a peanut on his nose." I moved aside to reveal my sweet dog. "Sit pretty, Keats."

Keeping his butt firmly planted, Keats sat upright, his white front paws dangling. His blue eye looked a bit eerie as he stared up at Lloyd. Maybe the dogcatcher thought so too, because he took another step back.

"Just keep your dog away from livestock, Ivy," he said, holding out the ticket.

I refused to take it and it flapped in the breeze. From the paddock, one of the cows let out a long, low moo.

"You're making everyone sad, Lloyd," I said. "Won't you please reconsider?"

"The ticket's already on record. No going back," he

said. "Take it, or I'll drop it by the post office and word will get around faster. Your call."

"The word's already gotten around, I'm sure. Everyone knows your truck. You're putting a black mark on my inn before I've even opened."

Walking down the stairs, his shoulders shifted in a shrug. "I have the feeling we'll meet again before long, Ivy. You take care, now."

I stepped back inside, slammed the screen door, and then slammed the wooden door for good measure. Outside the boots clomped back up the stairs and I heard the lid of the old metal mailbox creak open and shut. He had probably dumped that ticket inside.

The heavy footsteps moved away and I flipped the bird at the door. The clomping stopped, almost as if Lloyd could sense it. Finally he moved off, and then his tires crunched over the gravel as he pulled away.

Stooping, I gathered Keats into a hug. He didn't love being squeezed but endured it for me. "The fun's just beginning, buddy. Get ready for a bumpy ride."

CHAPTER TWO

I almost enjoyed the 10-minute drive to the Clover Grove Country Store that afternoon. It was sunny and warm, and the smell of green meadows and manure drifted in from the passenger window as Keats stuck his head out and surveyed his new domain. The dog had clearly put his past behind him, and I needed to do that, too.

Our ride was far from smooth, however, because the big black pickup truck that came with the farm had a standard transmission. My older sister Daisy had taught me to drive on a stick when I was 16 but it wasn't as much like riding a bike as I'd hoped. Sometimes the truck lurched and stalled out—always in embarrassing places, like a four-way stop where people could see me. No doubt it cemented their view that the city slicker should have stayed in her high-rise. But every drive got a little bit better and I liked riding above the crowd. Or as much above the crowd as you could be in an area where everyone seemed to drive trucks.

From the outside, Myrtle's Store—as the Clover Grove Country Store was more commonly known— looked like it hadn't changed a bit since I came with my brother and sisters for penny candy long ago. The big green sign with its ornate gold lettering had a quaint charm, and the fresh white paint made it look well cared for. It *was* well cared for by Myrtle McCain, who'd been running the store for nearly 50 years, after taking over from her dad, and his dad before him. The store was older than Wolff County itself and was something people could rely on in a changing landscape.

Inside, Myrtle's Store was a curious mix of the old and the new. Some of the shelves held dusty old hardware supplies and fishing gear that may have predated my existence. Behind the cash register, however, hung cell phones, and electric razors and toothbrushes. There was a clear plastic shield over the counter that covered rows of lottery tickets and calling cards. The penny candy had been replaced by racks of chocolate bars, some imported from Europe. Myrtle would order in almost anything you wanted, which is why there was such a haphazard array of products in the grocery aisles.

A couple of years ago, she'd installed a long laminate bar along the wide front window. The stools were rarely empty. Clover Glove residents hoisted themselves up to watch the local traffic and enjoy a good cup of coffee. The makeshift café was meant as a showcase for Myrtle's granddaughter, Mandy, who was a gifted baker. They rotated through a long list of tasty treats. If you really wanted a lemon square, you came before noon on Tuesday, because they were gone by two p.m.

Myrtle's silver head was bent over a laptop when I walked in with Keats. "Ivy," she said, looking up with twinkling blue eyes and a welcoming smile. "You look wonderful."

That was about as true as what I'd said earlier to Lloyd. My hair was in a ponytail and I hadn't bothered to doll up for errands. I probably looked as frazzled as I felt.

"Thanks, Myrtle. You look well, too." In fact, she looked far younger than the 75 years she claimed. Some said she was closer to 80.

"Couldn't be better." She got up and leaned over the counter. "But I'm a bit worried about *you* and your hand-some sidekick."

I expected this but my face flushed anyway. "You've heard. Honestly, I forgot how fast news travels in Clover Grove and all of Wolff County." The name came out as "Woof," like it did with anyone born and bred here. Pronouncing the "L" instantly showed you were an outsider.

"Oh, honey, don't you worry about Lloyd Boyce. He's a fool, but his bark is worse than his bite."

Lloyd and his colleagues in Animal Services were widely reviled in this pet-loving county. It hadn't always been that way, but the meteoric rise of a city to our west called Dorset Hills—known for being the best city for dog-lovers—had put pressure on Wolff County. Land prices had gone up because people wanted to buy close to the bigger center. Plus, draconian policies about dog behavior in the neighboring city had led to an increase in "problem dogs" being dumped in Wolff County. Our Animal Services had grown as a result, and their staff were trying to grapple with the effects of being in the shadow of a quirky tourist attraction.

"Edna Evans reported Keats for chasing her chickens," I said. "All he did was herd them off my property and safely onto hers."

"Gotta love the border collie drive," Myrtle said. She peered over the counter at Keats and his mouth opened in a sloppy grin of agreement. "Always had one myself until a few years ago. Can't keep up anymore."

I nodded. "This one hardly ever closes his eyes."

Since I'd rescued Keats as a malnourished adolescent, he'd put on nearly 20 pounds and his coat was now thick and shiny. Now just over a year old, his energy seemed boundless.

"And beautiful eyes they are," she said. Keats waved his tail, complete with white plume, to signify his approval of Myrtle. He didn't take to everyone, but she'd made the grade. Looking up from the dog, she reached for the list in my hand. "What can I get the innkeeper today?"

"Strike off whatever you can," I said. "I'll get the rest in town."

Myrtle cocked her head as she read. "Curtain rods... I think there's a few in the stock room. Definitely have a stainless steel Dutch oven back there, and yes to the portable vacuum. Not sure about the air pump, though." She looked up. "This could take a bit. Why don't you have a coffee?"

"Sure. What's the treat of the day?"

"Apple cheesecake's the Monday special. A personal favorite."

"Done." I headed over to the bar. Two of the five stools were already taken, and I chose the one on the end. "Morning," I said to the couple down the row. They were probably in their late sixties, with gray hair and matching, oversized glasses. After a quick nod, they went right back to doing the newspaper crossword puzzle.

Mandy came over with my coffee and a slab of cheesecake. She was slender and pale, with dirty blonde hair and brilliant blue eyes like her grandmother's. "Hey Ivy, you're going to like this one," she said.

"Everything you bake is an automatic yes for me, Mandy," I said. "I'll put on 10 pounds before the inn even opens."

She gave me a shy smile. Back in school, Mandy rarely spoke, but discovering her baking genius had given her confidence.

I took a bite, chewed and then closed my eyes in bliss.

"Should we put it on the list?" she asked.

"Heck yeah," I said. "My guests are going to keep coming back for this alone."

"Have you lined up any customers yet?"

"Not yet, but I won't start putting the word out till everything's just right. Daisy says I'm a control freak, and she's not far wrong." I took a sip of coffee, staring at Mandy over the brim. "Your boyfriend gave me a ticket this morning." I nudged Keats with my foot. "More specifically, he gave Keats a ticket."

Color rushed up Mandy's throat and into her cheeks. "Lloyd isn't my boyfriend."

"Really? He said you were seeing each other."

"We've chatted a few times when our bowling

leagues met up in Brenton, that's all." She leaned in so the crossword couple couldn't hear. "His divorce isn't even final."

"Okay, well that's a relief. I was worried you'd take his advice to sell the store and leave town. You know I'm counting on your baking to help build my name."

"Sell the store? Of course not." She turned to the counter but Myrtle was nowhere in sight. "I promise to keep Runaway Farm in baked goods for many years to come."

As soon as Mandy walked away, the older couple looked up from their crossword. They both had plump, kind faces. The woman pointed at Keats with her pencil. "Is this the dog Lloyd Boyce targeted this morning?"

I nodded. "Unauthorized herding of a neighbor's chickens."

I expected her to laugh but her eyes filled with tears. "Lloyd killed my dog, you know. Sweetest shepherd cross you could ever meet."

Her husband patted her shoulder. "Don't get yourself upset, now, honey. It's been years."

"Feels like yesterday." The woman swallowed hard. "I'm Margie Hodgson and this is my husband, Fred. I left our dog Gunner tied up outside the butcher shop and someone reported that he snapped at a child who poked him with a stick. There was absolutely no evidence but Lloyd Boyce rolled up in his van, snagged Gunner in a noose and dragged him away." She lifted her heavy glasses and swiped at the tears with her sleeve. "I will never forget that heartrending howl as long as I live. And I will never forgive that man."

"Margie." Fred Hodgson squeezed her hand to get her attention. "What's a five-letter word for Batman's nemesis?"

"Joker," Margie said. "Idiot. Loser. Lloyd."

"Sounds about right." The voice came from behind and I spun on my stool to see a tall woman with dark eyes and immaculately flat-ironed brown hair. Her jacket was high end, although it probably had some years on it. "That's my ex-husband you're talking about."

"I'm sorry," I said quickly. "I had an unfortunate encounter with Lloyd this morning."

"I had an unfortunate eight years with Lloyd." Her laugh had a bitter edge. "I'm Nadine Boyce, soon to be Tanner again. You must be Ivy Galloway. I heard about what happened."

I stood, careful not to step on Keats, and shook her hand. "Sounds like everyone has."

"I helped your sister Daisy buy her house," Nadine said, seamlessly slipping a business card into my hand. "If Lloyd drives you out, give me a call."

"Lloyd will never drive me out of Runaway Farm, but thanks."

Nadine smiled over her shoulder as she walked into the grocery aisle. "I hope not, but you wouldn't be the first. Keep a close eye on that handsome dog of yours."

When I looked back, the Hodgsons had slipped away. Maybe they didn't want to be anywhere near Lloyd's ex. I glanced out the window in time to see them wave from the parking lot and raised my hand in return.

"Myrtle!" A man stood at the counter and bellowed. "Hello! Myrtle!"

She hurried out of the back room, flushed from the effort of digging up the items on my list. Running a place like this had to be hard on a woman of her age.

"Why hello, Brian. You look wonderful today."

Okay, now I *knew* it was a polite lie because Brian looked way less wonderful than I did. He was probably only a few years older than me, yet his beard was graying. His hair was thinning and he'd tied what was left in a scraggly ponytail. That was never a good look on a man, in my opinion.

He grunted at Myrtle. "Did my package come?"

She shook her head. "I told you I'd call you the second it did. Don't I always keep my word?"

His shoulders slumped. "No. You didn't bring in the Vegemite like you promised."

Myrtle laughed. "It's coming. Hold onto your kangaroos."

He smiled and the mood lightened instantly. "Call me," he reminded her, turning to go. "Don't leave that package unattended for one second, okay? It's valuable."

"Promise repeated," Myrtle said. As he turned, she glanced over at me and rolled her eyes.

Brian had to step around a tall, heavy-set man on his way out. The guy was hard to miss, with his shaved head and tattoos creeping over his collar. Even from my spot at the window, I could see a bright yellow serpent twisting up and around the man's ear. There was a hint of red where the tongue darted out that made me shudder. When I worked in HR, I'd struggled to put my bias against tattoos aside in hiring. They were so common now, but to me, tattoos locked people down as who they had been, rather than who they could become.

"I'll take a cup of tea," he told Myrtle. His voice was low but surprisingly pleasant. "And the treat of the day, whatever it is."

Myrtle nodded. "Coming up, Graham. You staying?"

"On the run," he said. "Gotta get the shop open and make a few people scream."

She laughed. "One day I'll get you to tattoo a little sheepdog on my shoulder. What do you think?"

"Sure. For you, there are painkillers."

His grin was unexpectedly warm, but the minute he turned to go it faded and all I could focus on was the snake again. Until I noticed the blue scorpion on his eyebrow.

I was anxious to get going but Myrtle was still juggling a stream of customers. One rather elegant older man in a nice sports jacket came in for a package of cigars. She handed them to him with the usual smile, and said, "Here you go, Arthur. Staying for coffee today?"

Arthur glanced in my direction and his eyes dropped to Keats. "Not if you're letting dogs in here, now. Isn't that against bylaws for a restaurant?"

"It's not a restaurant," Myrtle said smoothly.

I swivelled on my stool to face him squarely and said, "This is a service animal."

Arthur raised one salt-and-pepper eyebrow. "You don't say."

His tone raised my hackles, and that in turn raised Keats'. I didn't have to look down to know because it had happened before. The dog seemed to know what I felt almost before I did.

"I do say." I smiled to take the edge off the comment. "This dog is best in class."

It was true that Keats was best in class in beginner herding, but our therapy dog classes had been less notable. He had his own notions about how to provide emotional support and mostly that meant keeping me too busy to think. It was a valid plan and worked for the most part.

Arthur gave a little smirk. "Well, I'm not sharing counter space with a dog showing its fangs."

"He is not!" I didn't dare look at Keats. I was 100 percent sure his fangs weren't showing and I wouldn't give this guy the pleasure of showing doubt.

"Fine, I just don't want dog hair in my cheesecake." He accepted the container Myrtle handed him. "You and Fido have a good day, now."

I glared after him as he slid behind the wheel of his Mercedes.

"Never mind Arthur," Nadine Boyce said, coming back and perching on the stool beside me. The grocery basket she set on the floor at her feet held a quart of milk, cheese, tinned chickpeas and what looked like a box of rat poison. "His bark is worse than his bite."

"That's what people say about Lloyd," I told her.

"Well, *that's* a polite lie," Nadine said, smiling. "Lloyd's bite will leave you festering and in need of amputation. At least that's how I'm handling it."

I couldn't help smiling back. "I know divorce is never easy, especially in a small town."

Nadine nodded, shifting to let Myrtle collect the newspapers the Hodgsons had left in their hurry to go. "You've really got to think things through before you make the cut. It can get ugly fast."

I looked over my shoulder, wondering if she knew Lloyd had lined up her replacement already. Mandy had disappeared into the back room, possibly embarrassed to have so many people dissing Lloyd. But if she wanted to date the dogcatcher, she was going to need thicker skin.

"It sounds like your business is thriving," I said, to change the subject. "I absolutely love Daisy's house and she couldn't be happier."

Nadine beamed. "That is so nice to hear. Say hi to her for me."

"Will do." I slid off the stool. "We're meeting later to choose curtains for the inn." I picked up Keats' leash and he danced at the end of it, relieved to get moving.

"You've got my card?" she said.

I patted my bag. "But really, there's no way I'd ever sell Runaway Farm."

"That's what the last owner said." Her eyes crinkled. "Some say it's cursed, but I don't believe in that kind of thing."

A shiver ran down my spine and Keats pressed closer, whining almost inaudibly.

"Then I'd better pick up some sage and burn it tonight," I said, heading for the cash register. "Daisy said it'll flush out anything but your septic system."

CHAPTER THREE

"Do not let Nadine Boyce scare you," my sister said, towing me around the biggest department store in Clover Grove. In fact, it was the only legit department store, and its selection was eclectic and dated. Luckily, Daisy had a way of seeing something unique and stylish in what looked dull and boring to me.

"I won't," I said, trailing after her. Of all the tasks involved in getting an inn up and running, interior design was the one I hated most. I wasn't fazed at all by mucking out stalls when Charlie, my farm manager, was off duty. But take me to a department store and my throat practically seized. I was suffocating.

"Is that you panting, or Keats?" Daisy asked, keeping her eyes on the drapery panels hanging on tall racks.

"Both. We don't like being trapped inside." I paced back and forth, and Keats followed, staring up at me with his brown eye—the sympathetic one. "Do we, buddy?"

Keats offered his mumbled agreement. He always had plenty to say, even if I didn't understand all of it.

"You worked in a corporate cubicle for ten years, Ivy," Daisy said. She gave me a look without even turning her head. I didn't need to see it to know it was there. My older sister had been giving me the same look of incredulous disgust for the 33 years I was on the planet. She was the eldest in our family of six kids, and the first recipient of Mom's flora-themed names. After her came Lily, Poppy and Violet, golden boy Asher, and finally me. Mom's name was Dahlia, and she was about as subtle as the showiest variety.

"I've escaped all that now," I said. "Remember the year I crisscrossed the country firing people? My boss called me the grim reaper."

"You paid your dues and collected your bonus." She carried two curtain panels over to a window to inspect them in natural light. "Nothing to be ashamed of."

Daisy was always practical. I guess she had to be, looking after us while Mom worked overtime in a series of low-paying jobs. My sister's hair was even darker than mine, but already more salt than pepper. We'd probably aged her prematurely, and then her own kids—two sets of twin boys—finished the job.

"I'm not ashamed. Just happy to be out of there." I stared at the fabric she waved under my nose. "Daisy, they all look the same to me."

This time her look of disgust hit me head on. "The same! One is silver and one is pewter."

"It's two shades of gray." I grinned sheepishly. "Maybe my vision was affected in the accident."

My sister pinned me with hazel eyes that were also a

little darker than mine. "That wasn't an accident. It was a violent attack that almost killed you."

I tried to hold in the shudder. Daisy was the only one who spoke plainly in our family. Sometimes it seemed like she was the only one who spoke plainly in all of Clover Grove. I valued her honesty, but more so when it was directed at someone else. Especially Asher.

"It didn't kill me. And no matter what the cost, it was worth it to save Keats."

Her eyes turned into sharp points. "I know you adore this dog, but rescuing him single-handedly from a felon wasn't your smartest move."

"I wasn't alone. I had Jilly," I said. "And I don't regret it one bit."

"Ivy. That guy almost bashed your brains in, and you haven't recovered fully yet. It's not something to be cavalier about."

My fingers went to a lump hidden under my hair that was probably permanent now. "I'm not being cavalier. I just want to put all that behind me. And the attack, if that's what you want to call it, brought me the farm, too, remember. So it all worked out, right?"

She continued to stare at me for a moment and then her eyes dropped to the fabric again. "You've changed, Ivy."

"Isn't change inevitable?"

"Here's the thing," she said, walking back to the racks and shoving panels aside. "You've got to set a mood with your inn. People need to come through the door and have an instant emotion. Pewter will bring awe. Is awe the emotion you want?"

I knelt beside Keats and shook my head. "Nope. Not awe."

"What then?"

"I want them to feel relief that they've escaped the pressures of the real world, if only for a weekend. I want them to feel comfortable and safe, and ultimately tranquil."

There was silence above me, and I looked up to find Daisy staring at me with an expression I hadn't seen before.

"That's more like it," she said, crooking her fingers to make me stand. "How does this one make you feel?" She held out a different gray panel and traced the silver pattern etched into it. "What's this?"

"I don't know... an amoeba?"

Again she pulled the panel down and led me to the window. "Look closer."

I stared at the velvety fabric and tried to focus. "Is it... a pig?"

"Yes," she said, grinning. "Silver pigs."

I laughed out loud. "That's perfect! A mix of elegance and country kitsch. You're a genius."

She laughed, too, shrugging off the praise. "The truth is always right before your eyes. You just have to look hard enough."

Carrying the panel to the department cashier, she asked for a dozen sets of curtains.

"All the same?" I asked.

"KISS principle." She checked her phone and shook her head. "I always tell the boys to 'keep it simple, stupid,' and they mostly do."

I kept my mouth shut out of gratitude. Daisy's boys were sweet hooligans who spent most of their time wrestling, running or rummaging for food.

After we'd finished, she studied me in silence while we crossed the parking lot. I pretended not to notice.

"I'm not buying it, Ivy Rose Galloway," she said at last. All the girls in our family shared the same middle name, because Mom had run out of good floral options.

"Buying what?"

"This easygoing act. You've always had the worst temper in the entire family."

I laughed as I unlocked my truck. "Wouldn't you have a temper if you came last—after the golden boy Mom always wanted and before she got dumped by Dad? Anyway, that's ancient history. Do you think I'd have been successful in HR if I'd had a bad temper?"

"You drove it underground but it still pops up. Like this morning. I heard you got snippy with Lloyd Boyce."

I knew she'd find out but I'd expected a little more time. Daisy lived on the other side of Clover Grove, a half-hour drive from Runaway Farm. "Good news sure travels fast."

"Edna Evans called Nora Peters and she emailed Mom, who asked me to handle it."

I sighed. Three decades later, Mom was still delegating family management to Daisy. It wasn't fair; my sister had her hands full raising the boys and working three part-time jobs. Her real passion was interior design, and I wanted to help her get launched.

"What is there to handle? I got a ticket from Animal Services. I'll pay it and make sure it's the last one."

"You will *not* pay that ticket," she said, piling curtains into the back seat of the truck. "The County could bring it up anytime and prevent you from expanding or renovating. You know this farm's been a political sore spot. That's why the previous owner got rid of it."

"That's not true. Hannah weathered out the politics when the land transferred to Wolff County. Clover Grove has no issue with livestock."

"Not the typical farm animals, but someone's bound to raise a concern about the alpaca and llamas at some point. And that someone is Lloyd Boyce."

She spit out the name like it tasted sour. Like many people, she'd had run-ins with him over her series of rescue dogs.

I pulled the tie out of my ponytail and raked my fingers through my hair. "How about we cross that bridge when we come to it, Daisy?"

"You got a great deal on Runaway Farm, but you're pouring your life savings into it, too. You can't afford to have Lloyd ruin this."

"My inn will bring new business into Clover Grove. The County should be grateful."

Leaning against the truck, she folded her arms. "Clover Grove isn't like you remembered."

"I can see that. Now it's pies and jam and fresh egg deliveries. When did that all start?"

It was Daisy's turn to shudder. "I don't even know when the tide turned to homesteading. One day I realized someone had stolen our normal small town and replaced it with this sweet little village. And it is sweet, but there's a current of something else underneath."

"What else?" I felt a breeze on the back of my neck that made me hug myself, although it was a warm day. Looking down, I saw Keats' ruff was standing on end, and his ears pricked up.

Daisy just shrugged. "I can't explain it. You'll see for yourself soon enough."

I gave a nervous laugh. "Is this where you get woo-woo and tell me to smudge the house with sage?"

For the first time all day, she truly smiled. Daisy was the prettiest of all the girls in our family, and the rest of us weren't bad, either. "That's a good idea. Let's smudge the farm tomorrow when I'm over to measure for rugs. But you can't smudge an entire town, Ivy."

"Why not? We could take the truck for a joyride tonight and smudge Woof County."

She laughed out loud. "People would talk, and I wouldn't blame them."

"They always talked about us, and I guess they always will." I opened the front door and gestured for Keats to jump through to the passenger seat. The truck was tall but border collies came wired with springs. "I'm not going to be a slave to gossip anymore."

Settling her sunglasses on her nose, Daisy said, "Then you'd better stop annoying your neighbors. Edna's the queen of gossip and she's right next door to you."

"Message received. I know what I have to do."

She let her glasses slide down and stared at me. "You do."

It was a statement, not a question. As if I hadn't learned a single thing since she walked me to kindergarten.

"Yeah, I do. I'll take some jam and a few dozen eggs over there and suck up to Edna Evans. Pronto."

The glasses stayed on the bridge of her nose, telling me I'd missed the mark. "Like smudging, sucking up is never a bad idea. But that's not what I meant and you know it."

"Daisy, Lloyd said there was no way around paying this ticket. If you've got a better idea than jam and eggs, just tell me."

She gave me the "duh" look reserved for special occasions of sibling idiocy. "Let Asher take care of it. Obviously."

"I am not asking my cop brother to make my Animal Services fine disappear."

"Why not? He's helped me out in a pinch and I know he'd help you."

Now I stared at *her* over my shades. "What kind of pinch?"

She sighed. "There was an incident with the boys and graffiti, down at Hoggs Bridge."

"That's all?"

There was a long pause. "The younger boys had light fingers. That's all I'm saying."

"Huh." I was surprised. Daisy ruled with an iron fist and the older boys were now fine young men.

"You can 'huh' all you like, but you have no idea how hard it's been with Reese and Beaton." She pushed her long bangs out of her eyes and sighed. "They're challenging."

I squeezed her arm. "It's okay. I can run this problem by Asher."

"You do that." She started backing away, toward her battered gray minivan. "Heading home now?"

"Nope. Few errands to run, and then I'm heading into the hills to let Keats stretch his legs."

Keats let out a little yip of excitement and Daisy said, "Don't tell me that dog understands English."

I slipped behind the wheel and scratched his chest. "Not yet but give him time."

She rolled her eyes. "Make sure you spread those curtains flat when you get home so they don't wrinkle, okay?"

"Got it." I turned the key in the ignition. "No wrinkles at Runaway Inn. Except the ones I'm getting."

"Oh, and Ivy?" Daisy said. "We treat dogs like dogs around here. Don't be that weird lady people talk about."

"I spent ten years as a paragon," I said, grinning as I put the truck in gear. "It's time to let my hair down."

WHEN WE GOT BACK from town that evening, Keats and I took a walk around the property. We'd made it to the trails above town earlier, but a chatty woman with a yappy Yorkshire terrier called Sparkles had slowed us down. As a soon-to-be innkeeper, I felt I had to be friendly with everyone.

Runaway Farm sat on about 20 acres now, and it was far deeper than it was wide. Past owners had sold much of the land, but what was left was lovely. There was a well-worn trail that wound around gentle hills and through wooded areas of deciduous and cedar trees.

There were four orchards, from ancient to middle-aged. The apples from the youngest were apparently quite tasty.

The sun was already low when we started out but there was plenty of light to see the path, and I always felt safe with Keats. He ranged out ahead and circled back to check on me again and again. This dog didn't miss much, and while he was always "on" he wasn't frenetic. At least as long as he got a good run every day, which was a pleasure for both of us after city life.

So when Keats ran out and stayed out, I paid attention. Then he started barking in a way I'd never heard before. I didn't like the sound of it and stopped in my tracks. There were coyotes around, and wild boars, too. Something sure had Keats rattled, and when I called, he only came halfway back, his white tuxedo chest shining in the setting sun. Turning, he raced back the way he'd come.

If it were a predator, surely Keats wouldn't lead me into its jaws. There must be something he wanted to me to see.

"What is it, Keats?" I called, trying to sound big and menacing. I made a mental note to bring pepper spray and my sheep hook on my evening strolls. A reformed city girl couldn't be too careful.

Coming over the last small hill, I found Keats running back and forth at the edge of a field that had grown wild since previous owners had stopped farming the land. It was still tall after a nice summer.

My steps slowed until I got close enough to see what

Keats was fussing about. Something dark was sticking out of the rye field.

When I got close enough, I bent over a pair of big black boots. The heels had sunk into the damp soil, and scuffed toes pointed to the sunset sky. Manure and hay was caked in the treads.

And unless I was much mistaken, the boots were still attached to the uniformed legs of Lloyd Boyce.

CHAPTER FOUR

"I vy." The voice came from close range but it had a hollow, faraway sound. "*Ivy*. Get the dog out of the way."

I turned to stare at my brother. He was the only one in the family with blue eyes. We used to tease him that the recessive trait that had won him the gorgeous peepers also hijacked his brains. Asher wasn't stupid, but he was impulsive and accident prone. We had all defended and protected him, maybe a little too much for his own good. An old boyfriend of Daisy's got Asher his job on the police department and it was a surprisingly good fit. What he lacked in brilliance, Ash made up in decency, loyalty and courage. When he bent the rules, it was always in favor of the underdogs.

"Keats is just trying to help," I said, watching the dog nose around in the field. "Don't underestimate him—he could probably solve this mystery all on his own."

Asher turned to a tall man whose back was to us both. "Don't mind her. I think she's in shock."

"I'm not in shock. I've seen a body before, Ash."

The tall man turned quickly and pinned me with eyes that looked darker in the dusk than they really were. "Really, Ivy?" he said. "You make that sound pretty casual. In my experience, seeing a body is always a shock."

Heat rushed up from my belly to the roots of my hair, and I turned away in case Kellan Harper could see my color in the fading light. He'd made me blush often enough in high school. In fact, he'd gone to great lengths to do so. That had deterred me from dating him till senior year, when he finally wore me down. I hadn't seen him in person since our "turkey dump" breakup during college. He'd only migrated back to Clover Grove a year ahead of me, taking over as chief of police after a long stint on the Philadelphia police force.

"I guess I am in shock," I muttered, snapping my fingers to bring Keats to my side. "But seriously, Keats might lead you to a clue."

"I don't need help from a dog to do my job," Kellan said. He turned to issue curt commands to three uniformed men setting up lights. The gorgeous sunset had become an orange line on the horizon that would disappear completely in another few minutes.

I knew Kellan and I would run into each other eventually, but I'd hoped eventually would take a lot longer. You'd think he would have been well over a high school romance by now. Unlike me, he'd probably had a dozen relationships since then. Yet from his expression, he hadn't quite forgiven me. I didn't completely blame him. For someone who'd gone on to become a talented HR executive, I'd done a poor job of breaking it off with Kellan and regretted it ever since.

But that was another time. What mattered now was that we were standing in a field together with a dead man. It had to be the most awkward reunion ever.

Asher gave me a pleading look and whispered, "Can you just not be weird, Ivy?"

"Weird? Do you think I'm weird?"

"A little bit, yeah. You talk to your dog all the time."

I gave him a look. "Everyone talks to their dogs. If they love them enough."

"But you talk to him as if you think he's answering back. *That's* what's weird."

"Excuse me. I think—"

Kellan smacked his hands together. "You two. Can you save the bickering for a family dinner? In case you've forgotten, someone just died."

"Sorry." Asher's voice and mine overlapped.

"I didn't mean to be disrespectful," I said. "Of Lloyd or you."

Kellan knelt to examine Lloyd and then recoiled as Keats crept over and tried to sniff his hands in their latex gloves. "Ivy, please. Put the dog on a leash. I've got a forensic expert on the way and he'll find dog hair in the evidence."

"I don't have a leash with me. He's allowed to be loose on my property."

"Not if your property is a crime scene."

"A crime scene?" My voice had a note of panic and Keats came over to me of his own accord. "I thought Lloyd had a heart attack or something."

When I found Lloyd in the field, I'd stooped to touch his exposed bare shin, where his uniform pant leg had ridden up. His skin was cool enough to send me reeling backwards and groping for my phone. Then I ran back to wait for the police on the driveway so that I could usher them to the spot where Lloyd had collapsed. In between, I'd shut out the anxious thoughts the way I usually did now: by focussing on Keats. He didn't leave my side until my heart rate subsided and my fingers left the soft fur between his floppy ears. But the moment he deemed me "stable," he started his own investigation.

"It's a crime scene," Kellan said. He stood up and unbuckled his belt while I tried not to stare. Then he yanked it out of the loops and handed it to me. "Tie the dog up."

I did as he instructed, and then asked, "How did Lloyd die?"

"It definitely wasn't a heart attack," Asher said. He made a dramatic gesture circling his neck and pretended to choke himself.

"Oh my god, Lloyd was strangled?" I said. "On my property?"

"Asher," Kellan said. "Could you take your sister up to the house? There's no need for her to see any of this."

The cows were complaining in their pasture, reminding me that I hadn't done my chores. Most evenings I put the livestock to bed after Charlie went home. "I've got to feed and water my animals. I can find my way alone."

Kellan looked up at me from a crouch. "No doubt. But I'd prefer you had company right now. Asher can see you to the house and the cows will need to wait a bit. We'll come up to the house when we're done to chat."

"Okay. There's plenty of pie," I said. He started to speak and I raised my hand. "Fine. Understood. It's not a pie sort of occasion. Give me a break, Kellan. When you release your crime scene etiquette book, I'll be the first to read it."

The first of the big lights came on in time to show his lips twitching into a half smile. "You do that."

"Ivy." Asher pretended to zip his lip. "Let's just take the dog and go."

"Come on, Keats," I said. "If they don't want your help, it's their loss."

"Don't discuss the case," Kellan called after us. "You can bicker about the dog if you like."

"Thanks, Chief Harper," I called back. "Put that in the guide, too."

As we trudged up to the barn in silence, Keats kept turning back, always to the right with his blue eye, as if that were his crime-solving eye. I would have expected him to be unnerved by the body, perhaps even traumatized given the violence we'd experienced together a few months earlier. Instead, he was genuinely curious, maybe even officious. Like any border collie, he liked having a job to do.

Asher saw me into the house and I locked the door after he left. Was there a murderer on the property now? Was he watching me? Were my animals safe? And why on earth did he choose to kill Lloyd Boyce on my property, of all places? And what had made him want to kill Lloyd in the first place?

They were all questions I couldn't answer, so I did the only thing I could think of. I called Jilly.

"Hey," she said, picking up on the first ring. "How's farm life treating you? Are you so chill I won't even recognize you when I visit?"

"Not exactly," I said.

I sat down in a deep leather chair that was way nicer than I could ever afford. Hannah Pemberton had left the place semi-furnished, and most of the pieces were luxurious. Daisy and I were filling the gaps on the fly and trying to make my cheaper style blend. The family room, where I sat now, was my favorite place to hang out. It was part of the new wing and had high ceilings, and large windows that looked out on rolling fields. Hannah's plants grew tall here and the hibiscus was covered in fuchsia blooms.

Tonight, the leather chair was too comfortable given the circumstances. I got up and paced instead. Keats normally stayed by my side but now he was standing watch at the side window, closest to the murder action. I walked over and unhooked Kellan's belt from the dog's collar and set it on the hall table.

"What's happened?" Jilly asked. "I can tell something's wrong. Is your head okay?"

"As okay as it normally is... at least the new normal." Jilly had witnessed the attack and stuck with me throughout my recovery. She knew my brain injury had some lasting effects that were diminishing slowly but might not ever fully go. On the other hand, in some ways my mind seemed to work better than before. My intuition and powers of observation were sharper. Maybe they had to make up for the deficits.

"Well, then, is Keats okay?" she asked. I could tell from the clicking that she was on her feet pacing, too. We did that often when we had problems to solve—paced together while apart.

"Keats is more than okay. He's fascinated by the fact that someone was murdered on my property today."

There was a long silence on Jilly's end. "You're joking, right? It's not all that funny, in case you were wondering."

"Not joking, unfortunately." I started from the top and explained all that I knew.

"That's terrible," Jilly said. "This dogcatcher doesn't sound like a nice man, but he didn't deserve to die like that. And why did it happen on your farm?"

"Good question. I'm hoping Chief Harper will be able to shed some light on it for me after his investigation. Otherwise, it's going to cast a long shadow over the inn's opening."

"Plus you may not be safe," Jilly said.

"That, too. But hopefully Lloyd's list of enemies is short so Kellan can solve the case quickly."

There was another long silence and I knew Jilly was scouring her mental database. As a corporate headhunter, she had a great memory for names. I'd probably only used that name once but—

"Kellan Harper," she said, triumphantly. "Your high school sweetheart. Are you telling me he's on the farm right now?"

"Yep." I headed into the kitchen to put on a pot of coffee. "He's out in the field working with a team, including my brother and a forensics specialist. I got sent to the house because Keats was too nosy. Kellan took off his belt and made me loop him up."

"You looped Kellan up...?" Jilly sounded intrigued.

I laughed. "I looped *Keats* up so he couldn't get me in more trouble. Kellan doesn't know how gifted the dog is, and my brother was embarrassed by my weirdness in front of his boss."

"Oh Ivy." Jilly laughed and then sighed. "I thought we'd put drama behind us, yet here we are again."

I liked how she used "we." She'd always had my back in Boston. On the farm I missed her dearly after only a week. My family could fill some of the gaps, but none of them knew me as well as Jilly did. Even more so now that both of us were dealing with some lingering post-traumatic stress disorder.

"I'll be fine," I said. "I've got Keats and Daisy and Asher."

"What about your mom? And your other sisters?"

"Poppy, Lily and Violet took Mom on a road trip to give me space to get settled. They practically had to hogtie her to get her into the car. But she's always wanted to go to Disneyland and they made my dreams come true by taking her."

Jilly laughed. "You've got some great sisters."

"I know, right? Especially given this new Lloyd situation. I'd hate to have to deal with Mom's theatrics on top of all this."

"Maybe I should come down early," Jilly said. "I wanted to be there for your big launch but now is probably better."

"I'll be fine, really. Daisy will be all over this, micromanaging. You're better to come and set up my menu closer to opening. By the way, you need to work on your egg game. Those hens are producers, my friend."

"I'll start experimenting at home. How about—"

"Jilly, I hear boots on the porch."

"Officer Hottie is there?"

"*Chief* Hottie," I whispered, hurrying to the front hall. "Talk to you tomorrow."

Asher unlocked the front door without knocking. We pretty much had an open-door policy in our family, which was taking me time to get used to again.

"I hope that's coffee I smell," he said, leading Kellan through the family room and into the kitchen. "There's a chill tonight. Fall's in the air."

I had set eight mugs on the counter in case they brought the whole crew, but only filled three now. Asher carried them to the huge round oak dining table that could sit 10 even without an extra leaf. I followed with cream, sugar and spoons.

"You're sure about the pie?" I asked. "Mandy McCain's blueberry is to die for." I covered my mouth. "Forget I said that." My face heated up again as I shot Kellan a look. "Honestly, things just slip out these days. I haven't fully recovered from a concussion."

"I heard you hit your head," Kellan said, meeting my eyes briefly. "I'm sorry."

"It's okay. I'm doing fine." I gestured around the beautifully renovated kitchen with all the bells and whistles. "Better than fine. If not for the head injury, I wouldn't have all this."

Asher glanced around. "It's pretty sweet, but you're taking on a lot, Ivy. We're not from farming stock."

"I'm a quick study," I said. "Plus, with my HR background, I know how to hire good help. I'm interviewing tomorrow."

Kellan cleared his throat as he sat down at the table. "It's great to catch up, but we need to talk about Lloyd."

I nodded. "You'll have heard that he came to the door this morning and issued me this." I pushed the orange ticket across the table to him. "Edna Evans reported Keats for herding her chickens onto her front porch."

Kellan looked like he was fighting a grin as he took a photo of the ticket with his phone.

Asher didn't bother fighting his smile. "Edna's a piece of work. She's constantly calling in complaints."

"Asher." Kellan's expression was a mild rebuke. "Business."

Ash gave him a sheepish look and gulped his coffee before speaking again. "Ivy, tell us exactly what happened with Lloyd."

Pushing my hair off my forehead, I sighed. "It already seems so long ago. We had words. I defended Keats and asked Lloyd not to fine me, because it would put a blot on my record with the County before I've even opened the inn. He did it anyway."

Asher muttered something unflattering under his breath until Kellan looked up from the notepad where he was scribbling and gave him another warning look.

"Did Lloyd give you any reason to think he was stressed or upset at the time?" Kellan asked.

I shook my head. "No, although he looked a bit haggard. I hadn't seen him since high school and I was surprised at how much older he looked. Must be all the time in the sun."

Kellan took notes steadily and I had to stop myself from rambling on just to fill the gap. I never used to ramble. Until two months ago, I was a woman of few words and all of them sensible. Now when I was stressed, it was like I had verbal incontinence.

"Did he mention any issues with others in town?" Kellan asked.

"He told me he'd split with Nadine. And then he said he was seeing Mandy McCain now. He seemed pleased about that." I took a sip of my coffee, already lukewarm, and then stirred the sugar that had settled in the bottom of the cup. I'd added way too much because my hand trembled. "Later, when I was at Myrtle's Store, Mandy said they weren't actually dating. So maybe Lloyd was exaggerating."

Kellan kept his eyes on his notepad, writing surprisingly quickly. I guessed he'd had plenty of practice.

"Anything else?" he asked. His pen stopped and his gray-blue eyes met mine at last. They were as striking as they had been in senior year, although now lines etched the corners. No doubt he'd seen plenty of things in his career to make him look that weary.

Tracing the grain of the oak with one index finger, I pondered. I didn't want to be cavalier about people's reputations. Word got around fast here, as I knew to my peril.

"If you know something, you'd better speak up now,

sis," Asher said. "The sooner we can get to the bottom of this, the better."

Leaning back, I crossed my arms. "Like I said, I stopped at Myrtle's Store and I had a coffee. Nadine was there and overheard me talking about my run-in with Lloyd. She said some negative things about her ex, and she wasn't the only one. Fred and Margie Hodgson weren't fans either. No one likes a dogcatcher in dog country, I guess."

Pushing his chair back, Kellan got up. "I'll need a list of everyone you saw today, Ivy."

I stood, too. "There's no way Mandy, Nadine or Margie could strangle a big man like Lloyd. He must have other enemies." I turned to Ash. "Even *you* had a falling out with him after high school, and everyone likes you."

My brother shrugged. "Lloyd was a—"

"Asher." The rebuke was stronger this time. "We'll do some digging and come back to you with follow-up questions, Ivy. With your inn opening, this is bad timing for you."

"Is there ever a good time for a murder?" I asked, trailing after them to the front door.

He shook his head. "No. And I didn't need my crime scene etiquette book to help me answer that."

His smile was genuine, though fleeting. As the two men walked down the front stairs and got into the squad car, I stroked Keats' ears.

"I know what you're thinking, buddy," I told him. "But it's better if we keep our distance. Get too close and we could get even more burned than we already are."

"Hey," I called after them. "What about my cows?"

Asher stuck his head out the window. "I'll be back in an hour."

"Get a mooove on it," I said, and then regretted it, as Kellan shook his head before pulling out.

CHAPTER FIVE

M ucking out stalls turned out to be a great way to clear my mind the next morning. It kept my hands busy and my mind free to ponder what I was calling "the Lloyd situation." I had no doubt at all that Kellan Harper was good at his job. I'd seen the writeups when I was shamelessly creeping him online before my return to Clover Grove. In HR, creeping was actually common practice; you wanted to know what your applicants did on their own time to make sure they didn't embarrass the company. So I didn't feel as sheepish about it as I probably should have. I just wanted to know what to expect when we were sharing the same small town.

Daisy had called three times since she heard about what happened from Asher. I'd assured her I was coping fine, although I'd barely slept. I refused her offers of company and insisted she go to work and leave me to mine. Her parting words were a threat: if I dared to get involved in the investigation, she'd move to the farm—

with all four boys. I assured her that my previous brush with death had been plenty for one lifetime.

The man I'd rescued Keats from was a dangerous man indeed, and the thought of our altercation made my heart pound and my breath quicken even months later. I'd come here for a safe and peaceful life, so the last thing I wanted to do was start poking around a murder.

But...

I had a lot at stake. Guests wouldn't be in a hurry to book a serene farm retreat with an unsolved crime and a killer on the loose. So if there was anything I could do to help get to the bottom of the Lloyd situation, I was willing to try.

"You okay?" Charlie asked, as he fed the sheep. His silver hair and twinkling blue eyes made him a magnet for ladies of a certain age, but he was determined to remain a bachelor. The farm had been his soft landing after retiring from an insurance company—if you called hard physical labor a soft landing. Charlie did; me, not so much. In fact, I wanted to reduce my time in the barn and pasture, which was why I'd lined up interviews that day with potential staff.

"Fine," I said, leading Florence, the old blind mare, out of her stall. "Just a bit of a murder hangover, I guess. Can you believe someone was killed here at Runaway Farm?"

He was inside the pen with six sheep and crossed his arms on top of the gate to stare at me. "Unfortunately, I can. Things have been unsettled all over hill country in the past few years. Even with the politicians playing nice across county lines again, people are rattled. You can't flip years of tension off like a light switch."

I tied Florence up so I could clean her stall. "You think Lloyd's death has something to do with politics?"

"Lloyd had a controversial public sector job." He shrugged. "Was his death tied directly to politics? I dunno. Indirectly? Maybe."

"I knew there'd been trouble here but I thought things had calmed down." I ran a hand down Florence's sleek side. All the animals were in great condition despite being rescues. Hannah Pemberton had treated them well. Charlie said she adored the place and had only sold because she'd needed to move to Europe with her husband Nick and their baby girl to help run her family's business. After our initial conversation, all of my dealings with Hannah had been through lawyers. I'd gotten the sense that the sale was painful for her to discuss. The massive binder she'd left with detailed notes about the farm's recent history, the community and especially the livestock showed she cared deeply. I was honored she'd chosen me to carry on her legacy.

My phone rang and I dug it out of the deep front pocket of the overalls I'd initially viewed with skepticism but soon come to love. I was glad to leave corporate suits behind; you could truly breathe in overalls.

"Runaway Farm," I said, without checking call display. "Ivy speaking."

The perky voice on the other end startled me. I took a sudden step backwards and planted my foot in Florence's perfectly timed dump of fresh manure. The caller was my former second-in-command, Keri Browning. When I left my HR manager role—with the insultingly small buy-out that barely helped fund this farm—Keri had stepped into my shoes. Even though I was happy with the farm, my ego rose up out of its bottle and spun like a genie at the memory of how I was wronged. We hadn't spoken since the handoff, because the company was normally adamant about severing ties.

"We miss you," Keri said, after the exchange of pleasantries. "I heard you opened an inn on a farm."

"Soon," I said. "Just putting the final touches on everything."

"You always were a perfectionist. Your records were meticulous, and I'm grateful for that."

"I've had to surrender to imperfection here." I stared down at my right boot, which had all but disappeared into the fresh horse dung. "But I look forward to sharing the farm experience with visitors soon." I tried out my marketing spiel on her. "The scenery is breathtaking and it seems like there's a country fair every week. It's going to be an amazing getaway for anyone who wants to escape the concrete jungle."

"That's exactly why I'm calling," Keri said. "You know how we normally do our team retreat down south? Well, we just lost our hotel because of a toxic seaweed problem. So I figured why not do something completely different and get the farm experience instead."

My eyes scanned the barn in alarm. "You want to come *here*?"

"We'd love to see you and support your new project. Can you accommodate twelve of us?"

There was no love lost between me and Flordale

Corporation. On the other hand, guests might be hard to find in the next while, and my former colleagues were probably good for a trial run.

"There's room at the inn," I said, laughing. "I've been waiting for a chance to say that. When are you thinking?"

"End of September," Keri said. "In three weeks. You'll be open by then, right?"

"I can do that. But you'll be in my first cohort of guests, Keri. I can guarantee good food, fresh air and fun, but definitely not perfection."

Wilma the pig chose that moment to unleash an ear-piercing squeal outside to demand her breakfast.

"What was *that*?" Keri finally asked.

"Wilma. My pig. You're going to love her. Think about the team-building opportunities with real livestock. I'll get creative."

Keri's enthusiasm faded a bit as we firmed up the details, and by the time I hung up, Charlie was grinning. "Those city slickers are in for a shock," he said, winking. "Especially after you tell them about the murder."

"I have a ton of things to sort out before then," I said. "Including figuring out exactly what happened to Lloyd Boyce."

I'D CONDUCTED a thousand job interviews before, but never in a barn while wearing overalls. Charlie had gone into town, but Keats was at my side, ready to pass judgement on the three candidates I'd shortlisted. Since rescuing the dog, I'd grown confident in reading his body language. Bright eyes, perky ears, lolling tongue and a raised tail meant someone passed with flying colors. A head tilt meant the person had something to prove but he was giving them the benefit of the doubt. Drooping ears and tail declared a big, stinky fail. I'd make my own assessment while he sniffed around and then confirm it with a glance at my genius dog.

I'd hit the jackpot once when I rescued Keats, and again when I was practically gifted this farm. Lloyd's demise in my rye field had just broken my lucky streak, however. There'd be no coasting for either of us.

"I'm versatile," Tina Hollen said, picking her way carefully through the puddles between the house and the barn. It hadn't rained in a few days but the gravel path had stayed damp. "I love the whole idea of an inn on a farm."

The sad look she gave her suede pumps said otherwise. She was applying for a position inside the inn, but I was hoping for someone more versatile. Someone who'd change bed linens, serve a meal and then toss out some scraps for the pig at the end of their shift. Maybe it was asking too much, but I'd aim high to start and settle if necessary.

"Wonderful," I said. "Tell me more about your experience in hospitality."

Tina offered some canned messages while I watched her body language. She flicked her long brown hair a lot and didn't meet my eyes. Her mouth worked like a puppet and her forced smile slipped away again and again. When Keats got close enough to sniff her, she moved away.

Fail. I didn't need to see the dog's tail drop to know it. But I had to give Tina another 10 minutes for the sake of her pride and my reputation as a reasonable employer.

"The only thing that worries me," Tina confided, "is that there's a murderer running around here."

I pulled out my poker face and slapped it on. "A murderer?"

She gave up on the effort to smile. "Everyone knows Lloyd Boyce died here last night."

"Everyone?" My voice had a raspy edge that made Keats tilt his head. Sometimes it seemed like he could read my mind but he was probably just a good observer of human nature.

"People talk in Clover Grove," she said, shrugging. "They already talked about Lloyd, and now he's really newsworthy."

Keats circled around to my right side and offered his ears for a scratch. Normally he walked on my left but when emotions ran high, he migrated to my dominant hand. All the better to administer emotional first aid. He might not have aced therapy dog classes but he delivered excellent service in his unique way.

"What did people say about Lloyd?" I asked. "I knew him in high school but that was 15 years ago."

"Well, they say he only talked the talk for the County and didn't always follow the rules himself." Tina looked around, as if the livestock might have ears. In fact, the two cows hung their heads over the fence, as if eavesdropping. "I heard he wasn't faithful to Nadine and she was kicking him hard in the divorce."

"That's too bad," I said. "I would imagine Nadine

will tell the police all about that. I'm just concerned that Lloyd... passed away... here at Runaway Farm." Looking up at the sky, I shivered. A cloud had blocked the sun and the breeze felt chilly without its rays. "I hope that doesn't scare off potential guests."

Tina shook her head. "Probably not. I'm sure plenty of people wanted Lloyd to... go away."

"To go away, yes, I could see that," I said, opening Tina's car door so that she could climb in. "But surely no one wanted him actually dead."

"LOTS OF PEOPLE WANTED LLOYD DEAD," said Joel Carter, a few minutes into his interview a half hour later. "He seized dogs that didn't deserve it. A lot of them. And that broke hearts."

"I had no idea it was that bad," I said.

"He was rougher than he needed to be with that catchpole. It was hard to see."

I reached for Keats' ears again. "What's a catchpole?"

"A noose on a stick, basically. All dogcatchers use them but Lloyd seemed to enjoy it like a sport."

"That's so sad. It sounds inhumane. No wonder people got upset."

"Tempers run high when pets are involved," he said.

Joel had a ready smile, a head of auburn curls and a can-do attitude. He was young, fit and comfortable around livestock. Plus he worked part-time down at the Berry Best Café and knew his way around a kitchen and dining room.

Keats declared him a winner without meeting the remaining candidate, and his tail beat steadily as he followed Joel around.

"This dog rocks," Joel said, bending to pat Keats. Normally Keats resisted premature familiarity but Joel was permitted—nay, invited—to scratch his ears. "That blue eye is like a probe. Good thing I got nothing to hide."

"Keats didn't seem to like what he saw in Lloyd," I said. "It sounds like he raised hackles wherever he went."

"True," Joel said. "But he could charm the ladies when he wanted to. I saw that at the café often enough. He even got them to pick up the tab sometimes."

I shook my head. "They must not have had dogs. There's no better judge of character."

"True again," Joel said, as we walked back to his beat-up old Jeep. "I heard someone nearly shot Lloyd once when he tried to seize their farm dog. Maybe this time they pulled the trigger."

"SOMEONE DID SHOOT LLOYD BOYCE ONCE," said Gwen Quinn as we toured the pastures an hour later. "Grazed his shin right above the boot. You probably noticed the limp."

"I didn't, actually. Why would someone shoot him?"

Holding up her left hand, Gwen starting counting. "One, he seized good dogs. Two, he caused trouble with bogus fines. Three, he lied and bilked good friends. Four, he fooled around on his wife." She paused with her thumb still in the air. "I could go on, but this chat is supposed to be about me. I want a job helping Charlie in the barn and field."

Gwen was likely in her early fifties, with short salt-and-pepper hair, and sharp brown eyes. She was the only applicant to wear jeans and work boots, which told me a lot. There was a no-nonsense air about her that I liked. Keats, however, was reserving judgement. He stayed out of reach with his head tilting from one side to the other.

"Gwen, I read your resume and you're way overqualified. Why would you want a position like this?"

Her smile said she wanted to pat me on the head. "You're new here, Ivy. Or new again. You'll see soon enough that it's hard to find work in Clover Grove. Many of us have to cobble a few jobs together to make ends meet. I work part-time at Myrtle's Store and at a vet's office doing cleanup. I've juggled up to five jobs successfully and my references are good." She looked around and took in a deep breath. "An outdoor job suits me perfectly. I have special expertise in sheep."

That made me smile. "How so?"

"I'm in the Clover Grove Herding Club." She looked down at Keats. "I have a genius dog just like this, only with two brown eyes."

Keats' left ear came up in partial approval and the tip of his tail waved slightly. She was winning him over. Apparently flattery worked even on genius dogs.

"We did some herding training before we moved here," I said. "Keats loved it."

"Come out to our trial next week," Gwen said. "If you enjoy it, maybe you'll join the club."

"Sounds like fun," I said. There was a low moo of

disapproval and Heidi, the black-and- white Holstein, pawed the grass. She was always the most opinionated. "If I can get away, that is. I have my first guests coming in three weeks and a ton of work before then. My main goal today is to find indoor staff, to be honest. Charlie mostly has the farm covered, but I need help with cooking, serving and housekeeping."

Gwen shook her head. "I'm already trapped inside more than I'd like. But when you're ready for a backup out here, give me a call."

I walked her to the parking area and thanked her for coming out. "I'll keep in touch," I said.

Climbing into her old truck, she frowned. "Be careful, Ivy. I don't know what happened with Lloyd, but keep your eyes open."

"Will do." Smiling, I gestured to the driveway. "Luckily, I've got a guardian angel."

She nodded when she saw the police SUV coming down the lane, and then pulled out with a wave. On her rear bumper was a cute little decal of a black sheep.

"We landed a good one with Joel, Keats," I said, walking over to the police car. "But what we really need is a chef. Because my cooking will scare the guests more than murder."

CHAPTER SIX

I smoothed my hair and straightened my overalls when I saw Kellan behind the wheel, but before I could get my game face on, the back door of the squad car opened and a blonde whirlwind appeared. Jilly Blackwood covered the few yards between us in three bounds and wrapped me up in a fierce hug that would have swept me off my feet if she hadn't been four inches shorter and 20 pounds lighter. Still, she was quite a force.

"You didn't need to come," I said, when she finally released me. "But I'm so glad you're here. Why didn't you tell me?"

"It was more fun this way," she said, grinning. "I got to call the police station and ask for Officer Galloway. I figured he'd help me surprise you."

Asher was standing beside the SUV with a foolish grin on his face. Jilly won fans wherever she went and my brother appeared to be particularly susceptible to her charms.

Kellan Harper, however, was clearly immune. He got

out of the driver's seat and looked down at the barn as if the frivolity was not only beneath him but embarrassing.

"How long are you staying?" I asked. "I was just telling Keats I needed a good chef. My first guests are booked and if I'm in the kitchen, more people could die."

Kellan looked at me and frowned. "Really? Death jokes?"

Jilly frowned back at Kellan, a rare enough occurrence, although he didn't know that. "She's been through a lot, Chief Harper. You could cut her some slack."

"It's okay, Jilly," I said. "He's writing a book on crime scene etiquette and I guess murder jokes are filed under the 'don'ts.'"

Kellan rolled his eyes before glancing out toward the meadows where his staff were probably still working. I didn't know for sure because they'd driven SUVs and a truck right into the fields and were out of sight.

Normally Asher would have jumped in to squelch me, but he was too busy gaping at Jilly. She was wearing a pretty sundress with strappy Mary Jane shoes, and there was a woven basket purse on her arm. Her hair was flowing in loose waves, versus her normal sleek blowout. I guess she thought that was country casual, but as her green eyes scanned my overalls and work boots, she almost paled. She'd been thinking upscale country inn, and the reality of a working hobby farm hit her like a ton of cow dung.

"I'm staying as long as you need me," she said, with a resigned smile. "I cannot wait to see this fancy kitchen because I've been upping my egg game, like you asked. Now, who are your first guests?"

I sucked in a breath and steeled myself. "My old team from Flordale. All 12 of them."

Jilly rarely lost her cool but today her face flushed bright red. "Ivy Galloway, are you crazy? Those people are vipers! Wilf Darby treated you disgracefully—and after you'd been a model employee for 10 years running."

"I wanted to leave anyway, remember? I didn't want to fire people anymore. I was tired of being called the grim reaper."

"They should have let you go with class and a great package after your stellar service." She paced back and forth in front of me until dust coated her Mary Janes. "Instead, Wilf used the media attention you got from saving Keats against you. He said you'd lost your judgment, when you'd just survived a violent attack. He let you go before you could quit. You could have and should have sued him. Then you'd have a decent nest egg to get this place launched so you wouldn't have to welcome vipers into your home."

Asher and Kellan stepped away from the force of Jilly's tirade but I stood my ground. "It'll be fine, Jilly. Better than fine, now that you're here to feed the vipers."

"When exactly are these vipers arriving?" Kellan said, turning to face me.

"Three weeks. That's plenty of time for you to solve Lloyd's murder, right?"

Annoyance flickered across his handsome face. In the bright sunlight today, I noticed the white scar along his jawline that hadn't been there before. There was another at his temple that ran into his thick, dark hair.

"You can't rush a murder investigation, Ivy," he said.

"It takes as long as it takes. My lead investigator is off on leave, so I'm shorthanded, too."

"Guess you shouldn't have turned down Keats' offer," I said, trying to make him smile and failing.

Jilly smiled for him. "This dog is a genius, Chief Harper. I wouldn't write him off like that."

"Great, two of you now," he said, shaking his head. "Anyway, I need to ask you a few more questions, Ivy. Shall we go into the house?"

"Ask me here," I said. "There's nothing I wouldn't want Jilly to hear."

"She has a right to her own headhunter," Jilly said, grinning.

Asher looked at me with dazed blue eyes. "She's funny. And she can cook, too?"

Kellan withered him with a stare. "Officer Galloway. You are on duty."

"What do you want to know, Kellan?" I asked. "Let's finish up, so I can get Jilly settled."

He took a few steps closer, and the sudden intensity of his gaze startled me. "I'd like to know where you were yesterday at approximately five p.m."

"That's when Lloyd died," Asher added.

"Where I was? Does that mean you think I had something to do with Lloyd's murder?" A flutter of panic started in my belly and my hand dropped to my side to find Keats' head. It was there, like it always was in tough moments.

Jilly flew to attack like an irate hen. "How dare you accuse Ivy of murdering this dogcatcher that everyone in the whole town hated." She stomped over to stare up at

Kellan. "She has more integrity than anyone I've ever met, and trust me, I've met a lot of slimy people. Maybe as many as you, although most of the ones I know wear suits."

Kellan held up one hand to fend her off. "No one's accusing anyone. I'm just asking a question."

"Jilly, it's okay," I said. "The sooner he gets through his list, the sooner we're hosting vipers, okay?" I turned to Kellan. "But seriously. You really think I'm a suspect?"

"It's called due diligence," he said. "It's your property and you had a dispute with the deceased that day. I need to ask."

I glanced at my brother and found his eyes on his boots. "You can't seriously think I'd murder someone, Asher?"

He gave a quick shake of his head, still avoiding my eyes. "Due diligence, like the chief says."

I turned back to Kellan. The panic was mixed with hurt. How could he think so little of me, after what we once had together? People don't change *that* much, even after 15 years.

"You must have forgotten I got scholarship offers from six colleges," I said. "Even if I were the murdering type, I wouldn't be stupid enough to kill someone right here when I'm opening an inn in three weeks."

"I didn't forget. A high IQ never stopped someone from a crime of passion."

"I barely knew Lloyd even in high school. How could I develop any passion for him?"

"Well, he threatened your dog." His gray eyes were

cool. "You're obviously very fond of said dog. I heard you were plenty passionate when you rescued him."

I glared at Kellan in silence then turned the glare on Asher, who flicked his eyes up long enough to shake his head and mutter, "Not me."

Kellan shoved his hands in his pockets and I realized I'd forgotten to give him back his belt the night before. "I know how to use Google," he said. "The story was covered by many media outlets."

"Okay, got it. You think I gave up my old life to start over in my hometown, only to blow a huge opportunity a week later. Over Lloyd Boyce."

"Lloyd Boyce could have been an impediment to your business plan. He was prominent in our community for his work in Animal Services."

"Prominent but not respected or liked," I said. "The people I interviewed this morning said Lloyd had plenty of enemies—some who shot at him. Why aren't you interviewing *them* instead of making spurious accusations here?"

Kellan's eyes narrowed. "You were interviewing people? Don't get in the way of this investigation, Ivy. It's official police business."

My eyes narrowed too. "I was interviewing people for positions here at the farm, if you must know. But all they wanted to talk about was the Lloyd situation."

Kellan had the decency to look sheepish. "Okay."

"That said," I continued, "I'll happily interview anyone who might be able to chase away the clouds currently gathering over my farm." I pointed up at sky, where the sun had gone in again. "This is the chance of a lifetime, Kellan, and I don't intend to let Lloyd's untimely death in my rye field ruin it." I paused for a second. "Did he actually die in my field?"

Kellan said nothing, but Asher's head twitched a negative.

Jilly spoke up again. "If he didn't die in the field, where did this heinous crime happen?"

Asher covered his mouth and coughed, "Barn."

"Asher, desist," Kellan said.

"You mean *deceased*," Jilly said. "Oops, another crime etiquette faux pas. How exactly did it happen?"

"Strangled," I said. "Or so my brother indicated last night." It didn't actually feel good joking about it. Lloyd had his share of enemies but that didn't mean he deserved to be murdered and mocked. "Ash, are you saying someone grabbed him from behind in my barn and choked him?"

"Outside the barn at the back," Asher said. "Forensics are taping the area off now."

"We'll need to interview your farm manager," Kellan said.

"Charlie went home early yesterday. I'm sure he has a good alibi, because he's a good person. Just like I am."

"Most women wouldn't be strong enough to pull this off," Asher said, looking pointedly at his boss. "Particularly if that woman tore tendons in her arm just months ago."

"I practically had to spoon-feed her," Jilly added.

"Must we discuss that?" I didn't want to think about the accident at the best of times.

"Just pointing out that the chief is wasting his time

grabbing at low-hanging fruit," Jilly said. "It's a little lazy."

"No one is grabbing anything," he said, staring at her. "This is textbook police legwork."

"Or an old grudge," Jilly said, proving his cool gaze didn't faze her one bit.

"Jilly, leave it," I said. "Just let the chief do his job."

He let out a dramatic sigh. "*Thank you*. And the longer you circle the question, Ivy, the more suspicious you look."

"Fine," I said, echoing his sigh. "I was walking in the hills with Keats by five yesterday. And lucky for me, I stopped to chat to someone."

He got out his notepad. "Name?"

"Didn't ask. But she works in town, so I'll take a look around today and drop by the station with her contact information."

Flipping me his card, he said, "You do that." Glancing at Jilly, he said, "Enjoy your stay. It won't be dull."

"Well, we agree on something," she said. "But I never liked dull anyway."

CHAPTER SEVEN

I f I'd been on the fence about exploring the circumstances of Lloyd's murder, Kellan's visit left me determined. I'd have to squeeze it in around my work to get the inn up and running before my first guests arrived.

Hosting a big group so early in the game was daunting enough. But hosting my former colleagues—mostly corporate sharks—was terrifying. Now I had a murder hanging over the inn and had become a suspect myself. I was confident my name would be cleared, but my colleagues would latch onto that if they could. Some of them thought my injury had truly scrambled my brains, especially given the drastic life changes I'd made afterwards. Murder would just make all of it more titillating.

"I'm not giving them the satisfaction, Keats," I said, as we hip-hopped into town in the truck that afternoon. "I shouldn't care about what they think, but I guess I still do. That ten years of my life meant something to me. After their stay, I'm putting them out of my life forever."

I glanced at the dog. He was sitting upright in the passenger seat giving me a good dose of his blue eye.

"Don't give me that look. You'd want to clear your name, too."

He turned to stare at the road ahead, managing to maintain his balance as the truck lurched. There were claw marks in the seat because of my erratic driving, but Keats took the bumps with relative grace, like a surfer riding a wave.

"We'll need to be careful poking around," I continued. "Kellan will get riled, and I don't want it to blow back on Asher. Let's be super discreet, okay?"

This time Keats gave me the benefit of both eyes and then offered the mumbling sounds that had earned him his name. I called him my poet because he was always reciting. Maybe he was cautioning me this time, but I doubted it. He was a dog that liked to sniff around. Border collies were bred to herd but they were happy to take on just about any job. Investigating murder was probably right up his ally.

"Thanks, buddy," I said. "It's a bit unnerving, but I feel better knowing you've got my back. And Jilly, too, although I'm not sure we'll ever get her out of that kitchen. It's a mess already."

Once I entered Clover Grove proper, I gave my full attention to driving. People were already talking about me; no need to add a rear-end collision to their discussions. Maneuvering into a large parking spot in front of Sneeze, the groomer that specialized in hypoallergenic dogs, I hopped out and Keats followed. I snapped on his leash, not because he needed it, but because people would talk about that, too. As a business owner and murder suspect, I supposed avoiding "talk" would rule my life now.

"Okay. So the lady from the hills said she ran a shop in town. She didn't say what kind, but it's a short strip. If we walk up one side of Main Street and down the other, we're bound to find it."

Keats tipped his head, as if reminding me about using my inside voice. I talked out loud to him a lot, and more lately. Sometimes I forgot how that would look to others, especially strolling down Clover Grove's main drag.

"Fine. Just use your nose, buddy," I whispered. "Find this woman so we can get an alibi. Find her Yorkie. Find Sparkles."

Keats used his nose, and judging by his posture, also his eyes and ears, and maybe even his intuition. We were only halfway down the street when he gave a gentle tug to tell me he wanted to cross. On the other side of the road, he stopped and sat outside Miniature Mutts. The front window had a gorgeous display of tiny ceramic dog houses and dogs of every breed imaginable. If I were the type to collect, I'd want one in every flavor. There were probably plenty of people in hill country whose shelves were full of these. The workmanship was flawless.

Stenciled in one corner of the glass window was the name Mabel Halliday, and while the woman from the hills hadn't formally introduced herself, a ping went off in my mind. Pressing closer to the glass, I confirmed it. There was a woman bending over a workbench, painting a figurine. I recognized her highlighted hair. Clinching the deal was the Yorkie asleep on the floor at her feet. Sparkles.

"Good boy," I said, backing away. "No need to go in. I liked Mabel and can't bear to see her face when she hears I'm a suspect. All we need is a name to give Kellan. She can confirm I was walking in the hills when someone saw fit to end Lloyd on my property."

Quick footsteps came up behind me and I turned to see Nadine Boyce wearing a simple black suit and sunglasses. "Does he answer?" she asked.

I gave her a puzzled look. "Sorry?"

"Your dog. I could see your lips moving from across the street. Looked like you were having quite a conversation."

"That obvious, huh? Well, thanks for giving me the heads-up. And yes, he answers, in his way. Just not with words."

"Well, he seems like a great dog and you're lucky to have him." Nadine fell in step with me. "Lloyd would never let me have a dog, you know."

"I'm sorry," I said. "Sorry about what happened to Lloyd, I mean."

She shoved her purse straps higher and straightened her shoulders. "Thank you. Lloyd and I had our differences, as you know, but I certainly didn't want him to die. Especially not in such horrific circumstances."

"On my property," I added. "I don't understand how or why that happened. If someone wanted to, uh, remove Lloyd from the picture, why choose my farm?"

Nadine shrugged. "No idea. Opportunity, I suppose.

Perhaps they were both there at the same time and things got heated."

I stared up at her. She was taller than I'd thought when we met at Myrtle's Store. "Do you know anyone who'd want Lloyd out of the picture, Nadine?" Out of the picture sounded so much better than "dead," especially when speaking with his widow. They might have been on the road to divorce, but still.

She shook her head. "Not like that. Chief Harper has already questioned me and I told him the same thing."

"I figured. I'm not trying to undermine him, but I'm anxious to help the investigation as much as I can. Because it happened on my farm, you know. I can't help feeling there's a connection to me somehow."

Lowering her glasses, she looked over them. Her eyes were bloodshot, either from insomnia or crying. "I doubt that very much, Ivy. You just moved here, after all. I'm sure you have an alibi."

"I do, thank goodness." I had pegged Nadine as the most likely suspect, but looking at her eyes now, I reconsidered. They looked so... tormented. "Do you?"

Dropping her sunglasses onto her nose, she offered a quick nod. "I was at my hot yoga class. Chief Harper will easily verify that, I'm sure."

"Okay, well that's two of us down. How many suspects to go?"

"Lloyd had a long history of annoying people. So long, in fact, that Chief Harper will have his work cut out for him."

My stomach sank. A long investigation meant my farm's reputation might not be cleared before the inn opened. I said nothing as we walked past the mishmash of shops on Main Street. Clover Grove was transitioning from old and tacky to quaint and quirky, due to its proximity to Dorset Hills to our west. Our town was now little more than a suburb to the prosperous, dog-focused city just over county lines. Some embraced that, since expansion had plenty of perks. Those were the shops with the pretty antique-style signs with ornate black and gold lettering. Others were less impressed, likely for fear their quiet, rural lifestyle would vanish.

Finally, I spoke. "You said Lloyd wouldn't let you have a dog. Why?"

Nadine directed her shades down at Keats for a moment. "He *said* it was because of his job and perceptions. If we had a dog and it was anything less than perfect it would reflect badly on him in his job. That he couldn't sanction other people's dogs if ours was merely average."

"Aw, that's not fair. No dog is perfect. Even Keats."

He gave a little whine, so high-pitched I hoped only my trained ear could hear, but Nadine looked up, startled, and her shades slipped down her nose.

"Did he understand that?" she asked.

I laughed. "I don't know how his brain operates. He's very clever, but he probably just picked up a signal from me and decided to talk back. He has opinions."

"Well, he's wonderful." A smile lit up Nadine's face and I could see she was very pretty, though understandably drawn right now.

Keats wagged his tail, which was a rare enough occurrence. He took life seriously, and wagging was generally for lesser dogs. I shifted the leash to my right hand and touched his head with my left. "He is. Nadine, I'm not joking when I say my life totally changed when I got him. Now that Lloyd's out of the picture, there's no reason you can't have a dog of your own."

"I suppose. I'm just so busy with my real estate business."

"Choose a small breed that you can take everywhere. Dogs are a great icebreaker."

"For people who like dogs."

"Who'd want to live here if they didn't?" I asked. "At the rate we're going, this town is becoming a clone of Dorset Hills—except people can still afford homes here."

"True enough." She'd brightened a bit, perhaps considering her breed options. Then her face fell again. "He was such a hypocrite. I couldn't have a dog, but he could have his pets."

"Lloyd had pets?"

"If you want to call them that." She shuddered, and her purse slipped down her arm to slap her hip. "I certainly didn't. He had a thing for reptiles."

"Oh. Ew." I shuddered, too. "I'm not a fan myself. What type did he have?"

"Snakes, for starters. One large enough to squeeze him to death. And some smaller crawlies." She crossed her arms and hugged herself. "Imagine living in the same house with them. My fridge was full of dead mice and crickets." Her voice sounded a little strangled as she added, "I moved out when the tarantula moved in. Even though he'd built what he called a 'safe room.' I certainly never felt safe."

"Where was this safe room? In the basement?"

She nodded. "With a secret panel." After a pause she raised her eyebrows over the shades. "These weren't exactly legal pets, you see."

"No?" I was grateful then for my well-honed ability to keep my voice neutral. "I suppose he encountered some exotic creatures in his work."

"You say exotic, I say revolting. Lloyd was so fascinated that he couldn't surrender them." She shoved her purse back onto her shoulder and picked up the pace. "That's why he was a hypocrite. One rule for him and another for everyone else."

I picked up my pace, too. "Well, I'm sure Chief Harper will have the reptilian menagerie removed and you can sell the house. A dog will go far to erase these bad memories."

Her jaw set in a way that told me she hadn't shared news of the reptiles with the police. Perhaps she worried about how Lloyd's behavior would affect her reputation and business. Or perhaps she just had such a grudge against the creatures that she wanted them to die.

"I'd appreciate it if you didn't mention this to the police," she said at last. "I don't really want people to know about Lloyd's secret zoo just yet. There will be an uproar when people realize his double standard, and that will reflect on me, because I didn't turn him in. I'll look like a hypocrite myself, even though it was all his doing."

"I see."

"People might not trust me in business, when really one has nothing to do with the other."

Time for a corporate dodge and weave. "Reptiles

elicit such strong reactions. I can see that story would travel quickly."

"Ivy." Nadine grabbed my arm. "I'm going to dispose of them myself, just as soon as I research how to do it without getting killed in the process. Then it won't affect my reputation or the value of my property."

"But in the meantime, they might starve, Nadine. Have you fed them, at least?"

"I am not going in there until my nerves settle and I know what I'm doing."

I sighed. "I'm no fan of reptiles, but I'll do it for you. Just tell me where to find the key and the safe room."

The shades came right off and she made a move to hug me. Luckily Keats was in the way and he didn't give her space. Neither of us enjoyed public displays of affection, outside of our small inner circle.

"I can't tell you how much I appreciate this," she said. "I promise when you're ready to sell Runaway Farm that I'll make it so worth your while."

"I'll never sell Runaway Farm," I said. "I'm working hard to clear its reputation and I'd appreciate anything you can do to help. The sooner this mystery is solved, the better."

"Chief Harper will get to the bottom of it quickly, I'm sure." Nadine stopped at the corner and people flowed around us, blatantly staring. "You two were an item once, I heard."

Heat rushed toward my hairline, proving my poker face didn't hold up to romantic scrutiny. "We dated for a bit in high school, that's all."

"Well, I hope things turn out better for you than they

did for me," Nadine said, straightening her shoulders again and replacing her shades. "I guess it couldn't get much worse. My husband was murdered and everyone thinks I did it. Or at least arranged it."

"That's not true," I said. "Some people think *I* did it."

She ignored that. "As you can imagine, my business calls are already down, and I need money. The estate probably won't be resolved anytime soon."

"Business will pick up as soon as they target a new suspect, I'm sure. Then you can buy your pup."

"A purebred West Highland terrier, I'm thinking," she said. "Terriers kill rodents and reptiles, right?"

"Sounds like a good choice for that. In the meantime, I'll pop by and make sure Lloyd's exotic treasures survive till you move them."

This time we both shuddered at the same moment. Keats also shook himself head to tail, as if he'd been doused in water.

Nadine laughed. "That is quite a dog you have there."

"I hope to say the same to you, soon."

An older woman gave us a wide berth, as if getting too close would contaminate her. She clucked disparagingly and then squinted over her shoulder. Keats' ruff went up but I murmured "Settle."

"So that's how it's going to be," Nadine said, sighing. "It was bad enough being married to a cheater and a corrupt dogcatcher. It took ages to get the courage to split. And now this."

"Hang in there, Nadine. I have full confidence in Chief Harper figuring it all out."

She gave me a last, sad look as she turned to walk away. "Never put all your confidence in a man, Ivy. You'll be up to your eyeballs in snakes before you know it."

"You're probably right," I called after her. "I'll just stick with Keats."

Her right thumb came up over her shoulder, but she kept walking.

"SO THAT'S how it's going to be," I said to Keats, repeating Nadine's words as we took a stool at the coffee bar in Myrtle's Store. While I was placing my order, the Hodgsons had gathered their crossword puzzle and slipped away. Fred gave me a friendly wave from the parking lot, before driving off in their old red sedan. They were one of the few families in town who preferred a car to a truck.

Myrtle dropped off a huge helping of apple crisp with an equally large scoop of ice cream. "That would feed four," I said.

"You look like you need it," she answered, with a grandmotherly pat on the back. "Eat, girl."

"It's been a tough day. After a tougher night." I smoothed the ice cream with the tines of the fork. "I assume you heard."

"About Lloyd Boyce meeting his maker in your rye field? Of course." She perched on the stool beside mine, and I marveled again at how great she looked for her age.

"No one's too broken up about it, I'm afraid. Lloyd didn't have many friends."

"But I'm under investigation. As if I'd kill a man over a fine from Animal Services. As if I could choke someone even if I wanted to."

"Choking?" Her sharp blue eyes narrowed. "Is that how it happened?"

"I don't know," I said, quickly. "Asher was probably joking. You know how he is. That certainly isn't official."

"Well, you'll be cleared soon enough. And Mandy will, too. Your high school sweetheart has already called her to come down to the station."

"*Mandy*? She's even less likely to kill someone than I am."

Myrtle nodded. "True."

I wasn't thrilled that she agreed so quickly, but I probably had a reputation as a wild card after my dramatic rescue of Keats.

"Well, I didn't," I said. "Murder Lloyd."

"I know that. In fact, I'd stake my store on the notion that none of the Galloway girls could murder anyone. Maybe that's why your mom named all of you after flowers."

Keats had moved under the counter and wedged himself between my knees. The stress of the day must be wearing on him, too.

"Mom," I said. "Oh no."

Myrtle smiled as she got up to respond to a bellow from the counter. "Haven't told her yet? Oh, to be a fly on the wall when Dahlia hears about this."

"No need to be mean, Myrtle," I said, starting in on the apple crisp with more appetite than I expected.

"Just remind her no one liked Lloyd," Myrtle called back. "Remind her how many good dogs he sent to death row."

I chewed and the sweet oaty goodness lifted my spirits along with my blood sugar. "I'll send her to talk to you," I called back. "I'm already in the doghouse for buying a farm."

"You do that," she said, chuckling as she circled the counter. "Dahlia Galloway doesn't scare me one bit."

CHAPTER EIGHT

I expected Lloyd's exotic reptile sanctuary to be a shabby dump, but I'd forgotten that Nadine had lived here, too, until a year ago. In fact, it was a lovely home that reflected well on her job as a real estate agent. There was thick brush on either side of the property that shielded it from neighbors, but the grounds were lovely, with lush grass and large beds full of perennials. The landscaping was a bit overgrown, as if Lloyd hadn't been getting his hands dirty lately in legitimate ways.

It was still an hour or more till sunset but the brush was decidedly dusky. I drove a good way down the road and then backed the truck into the scrubby pines with difficulty, sustaining at least one dent in the process. It was pockmarked with past transgressions anyway, not all of them mine.

"Here's how it's going to go," I told Keats. "You can come into the house, but I don't want you in the reptile room. I have no idea what he's got in there, but if something were to get loose it could come after you. No way am I risking that, buddy."

Keats stared at me earnestly and placed one white paw on my arm.

"No begging. It's beneath you." I opened the door and jumped down in the brush. "Besides, standing watch is an important role. You need to let me know if anyone comes near the house. Don't be subtle about it."

He leapt out of the truck and gave a little yip of agreement.

"Good. We've got a deal. Let's get in and get out. Remember, if I scream, it's probably only because I'm so disgusted. Don't overreact and call in the authorities, okay?"

Forging ahead of me through the bushes, he turned his blue eye, as if to say he knew a real scream from a girlish shriek.

We emerged not far from the side door of the house, where a three foot high statue of Buddha sat peacefully on the small porch. It looked heavy, but Nadine had told me it tipped back easily to reveal a spare key. At least, if Lloyd hadn't moved it.

Luckily, he hadn't, and soon it sat damp and cold in the palm of my hand. Keats and I both turned to stare down the driveway, and then we both cocked our heads to right and left to listen. Now we were starting to mirror each other.

"Coast is clear," I said, pulling on a pair of rubber gloves. "I'm going to cover my tracks so that Chief High and Mighty can save his lecture for someone else."

I let myself into the house and used my phone flashlight to show me the way upstairs. I'd decided to collect the food before I went into the reptile room. There was a very good chance that having gone in, I might not have the guts to return with dinner.

The kitchen was as Lloyd must have left it, with a cereal bowl and spoon in the sink, and a mug with left-over coffee that was already clouding with mold. I paused for a second, wondering what someone would see in my kitchen if I happened to pass away right now. From a snakebite, perhaps. Then I remembered that Jilly was there making dinner, no doubt spreading the mess from one end of the kitchen to the other. She was an amazing cook, but orderly, she was not.

A cold wet nose touched my hand as Keats reminded me of my job. "Right," I said. "Bugs and mice."

Opening the fridge door, I cringed. On the top shelf, three mice lay in a plastic dish with their tails draped over the side.

"Poor things," I said. "Bred to end up inside a snake. Do you know how similar to us they are genetically, Keats? Very similar. To humans, I mean. Not sure about border collies."

He nudged me again. "I know. It's not the time for philosophizing. Better to focus on the fact that there are three mice, and therefore likely three mouths to feed downstairs. These have been sitting here for a couple of days. Maybe I should offer them something fresher."

I was about to close the door and open the freezer when I noticed the plate on the bottom shelf. It held an array of baked goods, including brownies, blueberry squares and the apple cheesecake I'd loved.

"So it was probably true about Mandy and Lloyd," I said. "Otherwise, he couldn't get his hands on the treats from every day of the week. It's a shame he didn't see fit to cover them in properly when they shared a fridge with dead mice." I leaned over to see what was in the jar on the second shelf. "And crickets."

Again came the nudge. Keats' blue eye gleamed eerily in the dim kitchen, and I sighed. "This is dirty business, my friend. I regret getting involved." I grabbed the jar of bugs and then opened the freezer door. Sure enough, there was a bin of dead mice large enough to fill the whole space. No wonder Nadine had left.

I plucked three more mice out of the bin and put them in a clean bowl that was on the counter. My stomach didn't turn easily and it held steady now. The mice were just food, I told myself, like the oats I fed Florence, the horse.

"Let's go," I said, turning to head out of the kitchen.

Flashing my light around the living room, I groaned. There was a large cage of white mice in the far corner. Live snake food. I'd have to feed them on the way out.

Keats walked ahead of me on the stairs to the first landing, but when we turned down the second flight, he fell back, keeping close to my leg.

At the foot of the basement stairs was an open area with dark-paneled walls. One of them concealed the door to the reptile room. I took a wild guess that it was the one covered with Lloyd's high school award pennants—from his glory days, before he became a pariah. Stepping forward, I ran my fingers along the edge of the panel where it met the wall and found the little notch that allowed it to slide back and reveal a door. I'd feared more locks but there was just a simple clasp. Far too simple for what the room contained, if you asked me.

Leading Keats back to the foot of the stairs, I hooked his leash over the railing. "Stay. I'm going to be fine."

The little squeak in my voice made Keats tilt his head to one side. I'd trained squeaks and squawks out of my voice long ago, in my first HR job. Squeaks showed weakness. But surely the exception to all rules was snakes, not to mention other potentially poisonous reptiles.

I took a cautious step inside the room and closed the door behind me. It was bright inside from all the heat lamps, so I switched off my light and slid the phone into my pocket. A dank, musty smell filled my nostrils and the heat made me gasp. Maybe it was just the confined, seemingly airless space, or maybe reptiles stank. What if one of the three had refused its last mouse and it was rotting in there?

Over a dozen glass tanks in various sizes lined the walls, but the snakes had pride of place. Three large terrariums sat directly ahead of me, each of which contained a coiled snake. Two of the inhabitants were brilliant yellow, and the third was sort of a leopard print.

"Let's get this over with," I said to no one, since Keats was no longer nearby. "Three snakes, three mice. How hard can it be? Then a sprinkling of bugs to the lesser reptiles and arachnids."

My feet didn't get the memo. They stayed planted as I stared across the room.

"It's the right thing to do. It's not their fault they were born snakes."

Finally my feet complied, and I moved to the smallest tank first, the one with the leopard print snake. That one seemed kind of average, and less likely to cast a spell over me.

I moved the glass top back ever-so-slowly, keeping an eye on the snake. It raised its head and flicked its tongue but otherwise stayed in a tight coil. After a second or two of careful observation, I picked up one of the frozen mice by the tail with my gloved hand and dropped it inside. The snake pretended not to notice as I closed the lid, which made me think defrosted might have been the better way to go.

Snake number two was the smaller of the golden snakes, and it looked to be a good eight feet long. I hoped I wouldn't have reason to find out. Again, it did nothing but flick its tongue as I eased the lid back and tossed in dinner. Like the first snake, it ignored the mouse. No one likes an audience, I figured. Once I was gone that mouse would become a bump in a long log.

The snake in the center of the shelf was clearly the queen among reptiles. This one had to be 18 feet long. It was far thicker than the others, and decidedly less sluggish. When I moved in front of its domain, it began to slither slowly from one end of its massive case to the other. My heart picked up the pace in what felt like a primal response. Long ago, my cavewoman ancestors would have run screaming at that undulating movement.

Once it coiled itself over a rock at the far end, I braced myself to toss in the mouse. This snake seemed hungry and I'd have to be nimble.

Just as I was about to slide open the glass lid, something caught my eye. Directly underneath the opening was a piece of driftwood as twisty and oddly elegant as the snake itself. In the shadow beneath one smooth curve hung a slightly tarnished key.

I looked from the snake to the key and back. Lloyd was freaking brilliant. I hadn't given him nearly enough credit. This key obviously secured something of real value—something he didn't want anyone to find. And he'd left it under the watchful eyes of a genuine serpent.

Well, he couldn't foil me that easily. If this key could lead me to something that would save my farm, my animal family and my future, I would brave the serpent. I just needed to think it through.

I peeled off the gloves, pulled my phone out of my pocket, and tapped three words into Google: big yellow snake. The first result gave a positive ID. It was an albino Burmese python.

"Not venomous," I said aloud. "The worst it could do is squeeze me to death, and it would have to make a full escape to do that."

The big snake was a bit spirited, but as long as I kept my wits about me, I could drop the mouse at her end to distract her and then grab the key. All I needed was a stool to give me better access.

There was one in the corner that Lloyd probably used for exactly the same purpose. I put my gloves back on and set the stool in position in front of the key. Then I moved over to ease back the lid over the snake. Dropping in the mouse, I whispered, "Take it, take it, take it" as I closed the lid.

The snake waited a moment or two than then began

coiling around the mouse. Perfect. Hopping onto the stool, I took a long shaky breath. Then I opened the other end of the case and reached inside. Even with the stool, I could barely reach the key. Lloyd had much longer arms than I did. Standing on tiptoe, I finally managed to catch it between my gloved fingertips. As I did, the snake left her prey, perhaps attracted by the movement of my hand. She slithered with surprising speed for such a big creature and for a moment I was mesmerized.

A sharp bark outside brought me to my senses. I pulled my hand out, still holding the key, and slid the lid back. The snake's head hit the lid a second later, and my heart felt like it exploded. I fell backwards off the stool and onto the tiled floor.

Keats scratched at the door with a long whine.

"I'm okay, buddy," I said, leaping to my feet. No way was I prolonging my time on the floor in a room full of snakes. Picking up the key, I slipped it into my pocket. Then I hastily sprinkled some crickets into the smaller terrariums that housed an iguana, the terrifying tarantula, and various other four-legged beasties I didn't have time to google.

It was a strange day when a large lizard with spikes didn't faze me at all. Compared to the queen of snakes, this was a pussycat.

Keats jumped on me as I left, something he was normally far too well-mannered to do. "All good," I said, closing the door and the wall panel carefully. "Let's explore upstairs. Lloyd's got something hidden around here and maybe someone wanted it badly enough to murder him to get it."

Although he fell behind on the stairs to avoid tripping me, Keats circled me repeatedly when we reached the living room. He was trying to herd me out of there, to safety. I appreciated his concern but if I didn't take this chance I might not get another.

Aside from the live mice, which I fed with seed from a bin on the floor, the living room was just a typical man cave with black leather couches and a huge TV that probably postdated Nadine's departure. I moved to the first bedroom, where the pretty bed linens still showed a woman's touch. There was only one cupboard, and the door wasn't locked. Inside hung women's clothing, which Nadine had probably forgotten about. Pushing it aside, I shone the light around and saw nothing unusual.

Lloyd's bedroom was next, and my stomach, already queasy from the snake encounter, roiled even more. It felt terribly wrong to be here. Directing the light in a quick arc, I saw a big wooden chest and a doubled-doored closet —both candidates for the key clutched in my glove. Keeping the phone light pressed to my midriff so that no one outside could see me roaming around, I moved toward them. Then something on the dresser caught my eye: a framed photo of a woman with two small boys. Even in the dim light they looked familiar.

As I grabbed the photo for a closer look, Keats gave another whine, this time much sharper. It was a warning —make that an order. He'd turned to the front of the house and his ears tipped forward in sharp points. I heard the distant crunch of footsteps on gravel.

I didn't need to say a word. Keats led me at a run to the side door, and with my phone light turned off, I made my way outside. Signalling Keats to stay behind me, I crept to the corner the house and peered around. A man was walking up the front steps. While I couldn't see his face, I did notice a stringy ponytail. It was the customer from Myrtle's Store who'd been so pushy about a package two days ago.

Was it really just two days ago?

I stood motionless as I watched him scanning the place. He was looking for a way in, but he wouldn't find it as easily as I had. The key from the Buddha had joined the other one in my pocket and they were both coming with me.

Keats trotted by my side as I skulked back to the truck. Without the light, I couldn't run for fear of tripping and making noise. The bushes rustled and crackled as I pushed through, but when I stopped to listen, there was no sound of someone following.

Finally I reached my truck, and clambered inside after Keats. Locking the door, I puffed as if I'd run a marathon. Sweat dripped down my face and back and when I let out a long breath of relief, I got a full-body chill.

The man with the ponytail must be trying to collect whatever Lloyd had locked away. Maybe he wouldn't bother using a key to get at it.

But I couldn't worry about that now, because there were lights from another vehicle pulling into the driveway. Even from here, I could hear the sound of the police radio. I wondered if the ponytailed man would have time to sneak off into the bushes. Probably. He'd parked somewhere else, as I had.

Starting the truck, I pulled out without lights. Turning in the opposite direction, I watched the rear view, praying for two things: that the police wouldn't follow and that I wouldn't stall out.

It was only after we rounded a bend that I dared to breathe again. Then I turned to Keats, whose eerie blue eye was already on me.

"Here's what I really want to know, Keats," I said, tapping the glass on the photo I'd slipped between the seats. "Why on earth did Lloyd Boyce have a framed photograph of my sister Daisy and her boys sitting on his dresser?"

CHAPTER NINE

A delicious aroma woke me even earlier than Aladdin, the rooster, the next morning. Normally, all I could stomach before dawn was black coffee, if that, but when I walked into the kitchen and saw two fresh quiches steaming on the counter, I suddenly remembered I'd skipped dinner the night before. A farm girl could not survive on apple crisp a la mode alone.

"What are you doing up so early?" I said, brushing past Jilly on my way to the coffee pot. "You used to be a night owl."

She rested her hands, encased in silicone baking mitts, on her aproned hips. "That's before I had a purpose in life."

"You already had a purpose in life. You're the best executive headhunter in all of Boston. I can't even count how many great hires I got from you."

"I always hated that term," she said, turning back to the oven. Opening the door, she slipped in a muffin tray holding another eggy concoction. "Headhunter. It sounds lethal when it was really about glorious opportunity. Anyway, I'm looking for a kinder, gentler purpose."

I found a clean space on the counter and hopped on top, swinging my legs. Keats looked at me earnestly, angling for breakfast. I couldn't promise anything until there was caffeine in my system. "And your new gentler purpose is egg dishes?"

She smiled as she slipped off the oven mitts and walked over to the coffee pot. "My new purpose is helping you get Runaway Inn launched," she said, pouring herself a cup. "Dreaming up ways to use up your endless supply of eggs is just a bonus. And speaking of dreams, this kitchen is amazing. The granite counters, the six-burner, two-oven stove, the high-end cookware... It's everything an amateur chef like me could ever want, and I'm not leaving it anytime soon."

"What about your business? I can't let you jeopardize all you've worked for to help me chase *my* crazy dream."

She brushed blonde tendrils off her forehead with her sleeve. "I've left Steve in charge, and I'll stay in frequent touch. But even before I heard about Lloyd's abrupt departure from this earth, I'd planned to stay awhile. A deep breath of that fresh country manure confirmed taking a leave of absence was the right decision."

"You can't take a leave from your own business. You've been building it for ten years. And this rural adventure of mine seems suddenly ill-fated."

"Running my own business means I can do exactly what I want. And your inn is going to take off like a rocket, based on my breakfast specials alone." She clinked her coffee mug against mine. "Don't let a minor setback like a murder get you down, my friend."

Setting my coffee on the counter, I lifted my legs and swung around to jump off the other side. Keats followed me to his food bin and offered a full pirouette without my asking. After I'd set his full dish on the floor I told Jilly about my visit to Lloyd's the night before. "Can you believe he hid a key inside with the snake? Pretty clever, right?"

My words tumbled out fast because Jilly's hands were back on her hips, and not in a self-satisfied way.

"Excuse me? While I was slaving in the kitchen and entertaining Daisy, you were creeping in a dead man's house? Among killer snakes? Ivy Galloway, what were you thinking?"

I shrugged sheepishly. "I was thinking I might find clues about what happened to him. Nadine gave me the opening I needed. Literally."

"But you were almost caught in the act not only by the cops, but by a possible suspect." She swatted me with a silicone oven mitt. "That could have ended very badly. What if you'd been squeezed to death and no one found you?"

I held up my hands to shield myself from the oven mitts. "Keats wouldn't have let that happen. He can unlatch doors and he would have found help before my last breath was gone."

"Don't even joke about this, Ivy. You're a corporate HR manager, not a private investigator or a snake wrangler. And you broke into Lloyd's house. What will Asher say? Let alone Kellan Harper."

"It wasn't breaking in when Nadine gave me permission. I'm just more invested in solving this murder than anyone else." I hopped back up on the counter and crossed my legs. "You heard Kellan: he's down one investigator, so the cops aren't moving fast enough. I have less than three weeks before the Flordale guests arrive. Worse, every day that passes spreads the word farther across hill country. So many inns fail even without a murder hanging over them. It takes more than fine egg cuisine to make people feel relaxed and at home."

Jilly sighed and reached for a dish cloth. The mess looked daunting to me, but she liked to create chaos and then restore order. "You've got to tell Asher and Kellan, Ivy. This is no joke. You were almost caught by some guy who truly was breaking into Lloyd's house."

"It's Nadine's story to tell. Kellan's already interviewed her and she didn't tell him about the snakes. Clearly he hasn't pressed her hard enough. He seems to be more interested in pegging me for the crime."

Scrubbing a counter vigorously, Jilly shook her head. "He doesn't think you're responsible. You know I'm good at reading people. Chief Hottie's just doing his due diligence since the murder happened here. And he's probably giving Nadine a bit of time to adjust since she's the grieving widow."

"Well, she's handling her grief well enough to chat about snakes and dogs with me," I said. "I shouldn't even be on his list. It's insulting."

"Why? Because you were his first love?" She gave me

a sly grin. "Just because you were innocent then doesn't make you innocent now."

"Nice one." I grinned back, but it faded quickly. "What do you make of Lloyd having Daisy's photo on his dresser?"

Jilly's smile faded just as fast. "It's creepy. Especially if he was dating Mandy. She must have been telling the truth when she said they weren't serious, because if they were, she'd have been in his bedroom and seen that."

"True, but a selection of her finest baked goods was in the fridge, alongside the thawed mice."

"Don't even." Jilly shuddered. "Did Daisy know him well?"

I shook my head. "No more than anyone who's had a run-in with him. He seized their black lab when the first twins were small and she had to go down to the pound and beg to get him back. Then it happened later with their roaming beagle. I never heard her say a kind word about him."

"Well, you'd better tell Chief Hottie about that, too," Jilly said, turning on the hot water and clattering pots in the sink.

"I don't want him to know Lloyd was ogling my sister. In his bedroom."

"You mean you don't want him to know you stopped in and stole something from Lloyd's bedroom." Her voice rose above the running water. "Understandable. But you're going to need to tell him eventually. Your prints must be all over."

"Duh. I wore gloves. Do you think I'm a complete novice at private investigation?"

Turning, she blew away long blonde strands now frizzing in the steam. "Aren't you?"

"Officially, yeah. But these days you've got to do a fair bit of sleuthing in HR before you hire people. Seems like everyone has something to hide."

She rolled her eyes. "The people I sent you were properly vetted. And I certainly hope you didn't break into any applicants' homes."

I shrugged and hopped off the counter. "Do you hear Clara and Heidi? They're complaining about the service here. Time to get down to the barn and do the chores."

"Right," Jilly said. "All you can hear is the sound of your own resistance to common sense."

"That has a sound?" I asked, following Keats to the door.

"Come back in an hour," she said. "I'll have three different breakfasts for you to sample."

"You're hired," I said, opening the door.

"You haven't tasted them yet."

"Don't need to. Everything tastes great when it's made by someone who has your back."

"I'm not the only one. It just feels that way today." She came over and gave me a quick, damp hug. "Daisy said she's worried, and knows you're avoiding her."

"She'll have all kinds of bossy big sister advice I don't need right now."

"That she will. I got the brunt of most of it."

"Sorry. My family can be a handful."

"All families are a handful. And Daisy and I got on just fine after her initial skill-testing questions. I had to prove myself worthy of your friendship and then she allowed me to help her put up the new curtains."

"Oh my god. I should have taken you with me."

"No way would I have entered a home with snakes."

"See? I figured."

She stared at me with intense green eyes. "Snakes aside, Ivy, I want you to remember this: I know who you were, and who you are now. And I'll defend you to my last breath and spatula."

"WE'VE GOT A PROBLEM," Charlie said when I arrived in the barn. "Wilma's on the lam again."

"Again? I thought she'd given that up after retiring from YouTube stardom."

"Maybe she resents losing the limelight and wanted to cause a ruckus. You know how grumpy she is."

Wilma was indeed one grumpy sow, although Hannah Pemberton claimed the pig had sweetened considerably after having a litter, being spayed, and adjusting to a life of luxury. I still didn't dare enter her pen without what Charlie called the "pig poker," which was a long heavy wooden pole with a blunt iron point on the end. Grabbing it now, I went outside to investigate. Charlie walked around the perimeter of Wilma's pen with me, and Keats took the lead, as always. On the far side, the bottom plank of the fence had fallen aside, and when I leaned in for a closer look, grooves in the paint showed it had been loosened with a crowbar.

"So, Wilma didn't escape, she was set free," I said,

standing to meet Charlie's eyes. "Why would someone do that?"

He shook his head grimly. "That's what happened last time and it took all of the m— er, Hannah's friends, to find the pig."

"I know about the Rescue Mafia," I said. "Hannah told me when she interviewed me. She said I was 'Mafia material,' which I took to be a compliment."

"It is, trust me." Charlie's smile spread from ear to ear. "I was Mafia, too, before I aged out. Do you want me to call them? I'm still in good standing."

I shook my head. "It's not that I don't want to meet them. I really do. But Runaway Farm is going to be crawling with cops for a while and I don't want to put the Mafia in harm's way."

"It's not as risky anymore," he said. "With Isla McInnis-Duncan serving as mayor of Dorset Hills, it's been pretty peaceful. There isn't the same need for rescue."

"I have the feeling that crew still has plenty of work on its hands without dealing with my problems." I pulled out my phone and texted Asher. "Surely my brother can rally a few friends and help find an ornery sow. Besides, if someone's vandalizing the farm, he needs to know."

While Charlie hammered the plank in place, I propped the poker against the fence and started the search for Wilma. Although he wasn't a hound, Keats had a good nose and I trusted him when he led me off into the bush that stretched between the farm and Edna Evans' house. In fact, the closer we got to Edna's the faster Keats moved. He was so agile and quick that he needed to slow down repeatedly to wait for me. Finally we came to a large open space behind Edna's that served as a yard. Keats went into a point, with his front paw raised and his nose directed at Edna's vegetable garden. Sure enough, Wilma was enjoying breakfast on Edna's tab.

"Oh no," I whispered. "Get her out of there, Keats. And try not to trample everything. Edna hates us already after the chicken incident."

Keats dropped practically to his belly and crawled toward the pig. Normally he was faster and more confident but he seemed to realize Wilma was a whole new ballgame. The pig didn't even look up. She was grabbing greens, jerking carrots out of the soil and devouring them with contented grunts.

Creeping up behind her, Keats flipped the herding switch. He darted in and gave Wilma a little nip in the rump, startling a squeal right out of her. She picked up her hooves and ran out of the garden, moving with more speed than I thought she could muster.

"The road, Keats," I said, pointing. I was afraid we'd lose the pig in the bush, where the dog's smooth moves would be curtailed.

He swung back and forth behind Wilma, keeping her going at a steady trot down Edna's driveway. Finally we reached the smaller trail that ran between all the houses in the area. Most people used ATVs to get around and be neighborly.

Keats turned the pig expertly and we jogged over rougher terrain toward Runaway Farm. Everything going perfectly until we came upon a swampy patch that was apparently like catnip to a pig. Wilma charged around Keats, took his nip in her stride, and flopped on her side in the shallow, fetid water.

There was nothing Keats could do to get her out, or at least that's what he told me, as he planted his four white paws in the firmer mud on the dry trail and barked. It was rare for him to be so vocal, but he'd never been foiled by a pig before. Wilma let out a contented sigh and sank even deeper into the stinky silt.

"Oh, come on," I told Keats. "I didn't bring the pig poker. You don't expect me to go in there in my sneakers?"

The white tip of his tail fluttered delicately like a butterfly's wings at half-mast. At least he had the decency to feel ashamed.

"Fine. I'll do your dirty work, mister gotta-keep-my-toes-white. You totally owe me."

Gritting my teeth, I stepped into the swamp and gasped as I sank right up to my knees. Wilma was blissfully blowing bubbles, almost submerged like a malignant hippo.

"Get up," I said, pushing on her side. My hands disappeared into water so dirty you couldn't see them.

Wilma had the chance to do the right thing. Instead, she flipped in my direction and took me with her, deep into the muck. There was a terrible moment where I thought I was going to join Lloyd, wherever he'd gone. My inner rage surfaced before I did and I thrashed like a maniac. Drowning under a pig wasn't the way I'd depart this earth. Not if I had any say in it.

When my head broke the surface I let out a scream. Wilma, who was a screamer herself, did not like loud noises, especially at close range. It was a dangerous move, because she could have taken me down again harder under hundreds of pounds. Instead, she got up and moving again, running ahead of Keats, who managed to do his job while avoiding the splatter flying off the pig.

I ran after them, squelching in muddy runners and doing something my mother would have fainted to see: spitting like a baseball player. I had a mouthful of foul-tasting silt and there was no time to fret about ladylike etiquette.

When we approached the lane that ran into Runaway Farm, I called for Keats to turn left and he steered Wilma around the bend. Then she picked up speed, barreling past Asher's squad car and heading directly for the small crowd assembled in the driveway. Someone shouted commands and people adjusted position. There was nowhere Wilma could go without ramming into someone. She'd done that without hesitation before.

A woman in a baseball cap moved forward, brandishing the pig poker with skill. I wondered if it was a member of the notorious Rescue Mafia. They were said to appear out of nowhere when needed, ready to take on the most daunting animal-related task.

The woman in the baseball cap let Keats do most of the work but she used the poker when Wilma took a sudden turn and headed for freedom once more. The whack wasn't very hard but the pig squealed as if she'd been electrocuted.

There was a loud bang as the gate to the pen closed and an even louder cheer. I slowed to a stop and looked around. The woman I'd mistaken for Mafia was Gwen Quinn, and she bravely shook my filthy hand.

"Well done, girly," she said. "Pigs are much harder to herd than sheep. And your tuxedoed companion did a fine job, too."

"One of us is clean," I said. "He shirked his duty."

My brother unbuttoned his uniform, then stripped off his T-shirt and tossed it to me. I used it to mop my face and when my eyes cleared a little, I noticed Jilly eyeing Asher's six-pack. I suspected it wouldn't be long before he was invited in for the breakfast tasting menu. The way she cooked, he'd be down to a five-pack in no time.

"Gwen, thank you so much," I said. "You're a lifesaver."

"My pleasure, truly," she said, doffing her cap. I noticed it had a black sheep on its crest above the brim.

"If you'll excuse me, I'm going in to take a shower," I said.

"Not just yet," said a voice behind me. I turned to see Kellan Harper coming out of the barn. "May I have a word, Ms. Galloway?"

CHAPTER TEN

"Of course, Chief Harper," I said. "There's nothing I'd enjoy more than being interrogated by you as I asphyxiate from my own stench." I covered my mouth with a stinky hand. "Forgive me. The death references slip out like hiccoughs."

He shook his head as he led me into the barn. "I know this probably isn't a good time to talk—"

"It certainly isn't." The fact that he looked impeccable in his uniform made it all the worse. "Let's see how chatty *you* are after you've been rolled in a swamp by a pig and almost squished into the primordial ooze."

"That's never going to happen," he said. "Because I normally avoid farms. They give me hives."

"Then why did you come back to Clover Grove?" I asked. "It is a rural community."

He waved his hand as if a horsefly was bothering him. I suspected I was the real annoyance. "I called you in here to talk about the case."

"Well, I assumed it wasn't to exchange egg recipes, although I can definitely hook you up."

Stopping beside Florence's stall, he gave me a glare. That quickly dissolved into a smirk, which he tried to replace with a serious, professional expression. Then the cycle started all over.

"Ivy," he began, "I wanted to—"

His own involuntary smirk cut him off and he literally turned his back to stare at Florence while he regained his composure.

Keats circled between us with his tail going up and down like a pump handle. He didn't know what to make of the situation at all.

"Chief Harper," I said, with all the dignity I could muster. "Perhaps we could have this discussion another day. You seem distracted."

His shoulders shook. "It's just the... the smell. It's really quite pungent. More like sewage than manure. I'm sorry. I really am."

"Not as sorry as I am to be living in it. Chief, I really would prefer to speak after I've had five showers."

"No." He raised his hand. "I've got it under control. I think if we just stand a bit apart, I'd be able to focus."

"Of course. The more distance the better. How about I jump in with the alpaca and shout from there?"

"That's really not necessary."

"I have a safety mask, if you'd like. That might keep out the worst of it."

"No, really. I can stand it."

Just what every woman wants to hear from a handsome man. Someone who once found her attractive.

"Well, *I* can't for much longer. So please... get on with your questions."

Turning, he took a few deep breaths through his mouth without looking at me. Finally, he regained his composure and literally sighed with relief. It probably took a toll on his pride to lose it like that, which was a tiny bit of comfort given the assault on my own pride.

Keats settled in the space between us, with his back to me. I wasn't sure if he was protecting me or protecting his own nose. He had been careful to stay just out of reach since I left the swamp.

"You said you'd drop by the station yesterday," he said. "I was expecting you."

"I texted you the information you wanted about my alibi. There wasn't much else to say yesterday."

"But there's more to say today?" he said, catching the nuance.

"I'm not sure. Possibly."

"Then I guess it's a lucky thing that Asher made me come along for the pig party."

I turned Asher's T-shirt inside out and rubbed it over my face and hair. It wasn't much use now that the muck was drying.

"What exactly did you want to talk about?" I asked.

He stared around the barn, either to avoid looking at me, or to scan for clues. "Simple. I want to know everything you know about Lloyd's death."

Years of interviewing had taught me that "everything" was a broad term. It was better to offer only exactly what was requested. "I told you what happened. That I had words with Lloyd about Keats and refused to accept the ticket. He left the ticket in the mailbox and drove off. Then I drove into town to do errands. I stopped at Myrtle's, and I already told you what I learned there."

"Tell me again," he said, getting out his notepad. "You might remember something else this time."

He probably wanted to see if I'd trip over any of the details on second telling. "Well, for starters, Lloyd's wife said her years with Lloyd were miserable and she was happy to be splitting. Margie Hodgson said she hated Lloyd with a passion for seizing her dog with a noose and dragging him off in front of her. But she's not alone in that, apparently. Meanwhile, Mandy McCain denied being involved with Lloyd despite his telling me they were an item." I twisted my hair into a ponytail, and it stayed in place, anchored by mud. "I assume you'll interview all of them and don't need my help to flush out the details."

"I can do my own flushing," he agreed, with a twitch of his lip. "So then what happened?"

"After that I went curtain shopping with Daisy, which was torture for me, but she likes that sort of thing. I was glad to escape to the feed store. Then I picked up some groceries and went to the vet to grab tick meds for Keats. By then, I was pretty desperate for a walk in the hills, so I hit the Marquis Trail at around five. The light was still good. That's when we ran into Mabel Halliday, whose name I texted you, and her dog Sparkles. We chatted for a while about Clover Grove."

"While the dogs played together?" he asked.

"Keats doesn't really play. He's a serious dog most of the time." I looked down at him now and he was proving my words by solemnly staring at Kellan. "Did you speak to her and confirm my whereabouts?" I asked.

He nodded. "She said you met in the hills and talked for a while, yes."

I heaved a sigh. "Thank goodness. I hope the news of my innocence gets around as fast as news of my guilt probably did."

Leaning against Florence's stall, he finally met my eyes. "I get the sense you're not telling me everything. Did you speak to anyone else about the case?"

"Pretty much everyone I come across wants to talk about it. The young fellow I interviewed, Joel, he said he'd heard a farmer shot at Lloyd once. And Gwen, who was so masterful with the pig just now, said someone actually did shoot Lloyd in the leg and left him with a limp."

"And...? There's more. I can tell. Spit it out."

I leaned against the empty sheep pen and sighed. "Well, I ran into Nadine in town near Mabel's store. We had a little chat."

He rolled his eyes. "You couldn't just offer that up?"

"You're not offering much up, Kellan."

"I'm the Chief of Police. That's not my role."

"Well, I'm the one whose farm and future are in peril. Someone released that pig today, you know. Hacked her pen open with a crowbar."

He started taking notes again. "You see, this is the kind of information you're supposed to share freely."

"I would have. It just happened."

"Well, it sounds more like a prank, and Runaway

Farm has been targeted before. But I'll get Asher to check it out."

Pulling out his phone, he called Asher and told him to look around the pig pen and all the pastures.

"A loose pig is a loose cannon," I told him.

He leaned against the mare's stall again and ran his fingers through his hair. "Can we go back to your discussion with Nadine?"

"Have you interrogated her? Seems like she has a motive to me. She couldn't get Lloyd to finalize the divorce."

"We've had a preliminary chat, and we'll talk more. I know she was resentful over the breakup."

"It was more than the usual resentment. Lloyd wouldn't let her get a dog because he wanted to keep up appearances."

"I'm sure a dog can be a point of contention but—"

"A dog can be a dealbreaker. Especially when Lloyd was a hypocrite. Apparently he'd bring home rare animals he seized sometimes."

"She told you that?"

I decided to drop a few hints but not disclose the entire truth. If I told him that I'd been inside Lloyd's house, he'd probably make it more difficult for me to poke around, and I was determined to keep poking around until he resolved the case.

"Other people told me that there was one rule for citizens and another rule for Lloyd. Nadine is upset that Lloyd was stalling on finalizing their settlement. He didn't have the cash to buy her out. I really think you need to push Nadine as hard as you're pushing me. There's more to her story, I'm sure of it."

Kellan ran his other hand over his hair this time. Florence took issue with the flapping around her head and grabbed his sleeve. "Hey! Do you mind?" he said.

"Speak softly," I said, walking over. "She's blind. Your flapping scared her."

Now he was trapped in close proximity to me as I freed his sleeve, and he made a little retching sound. When I'd sweet-talked Flo into letting go, he backed away and said, "How about we walk outside?"

"Sounds good to me." Keats took the lead, and I followed him out the back door of the barn, past the big old red tractor that Charlie used to move things around.

Kellan walked ahead of me toward the goat pasture, shaking his head at their antics. They were a bunch of clowns, and hard to resist.

"Do you have any other suspects?" I asked, as we moved on to the sheep, who were so intent on their grazing they paid us no mind.

"No comment," Kellan said. "Now that I know you're a loose cannon like your pig, I'm going to be very careful what I say."

"As much as I enjoy being compared to my pig, I resent that, Kellan. I've given you some good information today."

"Not freely," he said. "And you shouldn't be chatting with people like Nadine, anyway."

"It's a small town. I'm going to run into people and make small talk."

We stopped near the cows and I introduced him to

Clara and Heidi. He nodded hello, and kept a respectful distance.

"There's a big difference between chitchat about the weather, and a deep discussion about a failed marriage," he said. "Not to mention what you're still not telling me."

"It's nothing she won't share herself when you question her longer. I don't want to betray her confidence."

"Oh, Ivy," he said, exasperated. "I'm going to give you just enough rope to hang yourself. But I'm asking you seriously to watch your step. We don't know what we're dealing with. Maybe vandalizing your pigpen was a message to tell you to back off."

I folded my arms over the fence enclosing the cow pasture. "I'd better set up security cameras. These animals are my responsibility and I care about them."

"That's a good idea, but I'm sure it will be fine if you just stand down." He moved on to the pasture with the alpaca and two llamas. "You shouldn't be getting anywhere near this investigation anyway."

"I'm just trying to help move things along. Every day this crime is unsolved is a day that my reputation is getting more tarnished."

"It's moving along in a measured way, just as it's supposed to. There's a reason we do things the way we do. If you blunder around shooting off questions you could fall on your face in the mud."

"Very funny."

He turned and leaned against the fence, crossing his arms as he surveyed the land and the barn. "Who else would have had access to the barn at the right time to ambush Lloyd?"

"Anyone really. It's not locked. Charlie left early that day and I was on call for bedding down the animals later. When I was gone, anyone could have come by." Goose-bumps rose on my arms and the dried mud cracked. "That's what freaks me out. It sounds like Lloyd just waltzed out here like he owned the place and found someone lying in wait."

"Or they happened to show up at the same time," he said. "We don't know anything more than that he expired around five p.m., most likely from strangulation. The autopsy report will be in tomorrow."

"Either way, it's scary. It was outside in broad daylight." I wrapped my arms around myself, clutching Asher's bedraggled T-shirt like a teddy bear. What I really wanted was to hug Keats, but it wasn't the time.

"You're not alone, Ivy," he said, and his voice softened. For the first time he sounded like the guy I used to know in high school. Only *that* guy could meet my eyes. "It sounds like your friend is staying till you get on your feet. And Asher is out here a lot."

"All the time," I said. "Because he has a crush."

Kellan's eyebrows went up. "On Jilly?"

I laughed and pointed to the fluffy, big-eyed animal who'd come up behind him. "On the alpaca. Alvina mourned terribly after the previous owner left. She'd bonded closely with Hannah's husband, Nick. Luckily, Asher is starting to fill the void in her furry heart. They dance together."

He stepped back from the fence, shaking his head. "I don't think I want to know this about my officer. And I don't want the rest of the town to know, either. It's hard to take a cop seriously who dances with alpacas."

Looking him up and down, I said, "You used to be more fun."

He returned the glance. "And you used to be clean. Times change." He was about to close his notepad. "Anything else you want to tell me?"

"Nope. How about you? Anything else?"

"Actually, yes." He closed the notepad and smiled. "Your neighbor, Edna Evans, called the station to complain. Apparently the vegetables your pig ate were meant to get her through winter. If she starves to death in the cold months, she says it's on you."

CHAPTER ELEVEN

I showered several times before driving over to visit Edna Evans that afternoon but I knew I still stank of swamp. Keats was keeping his distance, whereas normally he was a tuxedoed shadow I couldn't shake. Since the night I'd saved him, we'd grown inseparable. If I had continued in my corporate career, both of us would have developed severe separation anxiety.

Edna's face creased in a frown when she opened the door and it deepened when she saw the dog beside me on the porch. "I don't like dogs in the house," she said. "You can leave him in the truck if you want to come in."

"It's a bit warm for that," I said. "We won't stay long, Mrs. Evans. I just came to apologize. And deliver a pie."

"*Miss* Evans," she corrected, staring at me over her reading glasses as if to assess whether I was joking.

"Miss. I'm sorry, I forgot." Her pressed white frock, now yellowed from age, looked like a nurse's uniform and may well have been. For decades she'd worked for Doc Grainer, the town's only physician, and routinely visited the school to hammer vaccinations into our arms with barely suppressed glee.

Sighing, she stood back to let me pass with Keats. "People think a pie excuses everything in Clover Grove," she said, inspecting the perfect specimen I placed in her hands. "Peach. Out of season. Why even bother? There's no flavour at all." She leaned in for a closer look, her gray curls almost dusting the surface. "Pastry looks good, though. Gwen's been working on her execution."

"Gwen?" The heat of shame started a slow crawl up from my midriff.

"Oh, Ivy, I've been around the block a time or two. You're regifting a pie, and I'd know Gwen Quinn's style anywhere."

"I'm sorry. It was a lame ploy. There's nothing I'd love more than to bake my own pies right now, but there simply isn't time."

"Not when you're chasing your animals all over the county," she said, pursing her lips as she led me into the living room. It was just as I expected, with floral pastel fabric covering overstuffed furniture. The old oak end tables were polished to a high gleam. Only the fully-drawn, heavy curtains surprised me. I'd pictured her standing guard all day long watching for incursions.

"I feel terrible about Wilma," I said.

"Wilma?"

"My pig. Someone vandalized her pen and she found her way to your carrots."

Edna eased herself into a bulky recliner and kicked back. "Why would someone do that? A loose sow can be dangerous."

"So I discovered when she nearly squished me in the swamp on your side of the trail."

Edna covered her mouth but a snuffle of laughter escaped. "I'll have that filled in. What a terrible way to go."

"Indeed. And I can assure you that finding a dead body on your property is a terrible shock."

Her smirk faded and her hand dropped into her lap and found the other one. "Lloyd Boyce, yes. I figured someone would catch up to him eventually, but still."

"Catch up to him? What do you mean?"

"That man was as crooked as they come and I'm sure you know that. There must be talk in your family."

I perched on an ottoman without waiting for her invitation to sit down. "Asher doesn't talk about his work. If Lloyd was crooked, he never said so. They were friends in school."

"Oh, I know," Edna said. "I had to chase those boys down to vaccinate them." Her eyes lost focus. "I had some speed in those days. Most kids didn't just offer up their arms freely. You were a meek one, Ivy."

"Not so meek anymore," I said, smiling. "I was known as the grim reaper in my old company."

Her sparse silver eyebrows rose like seagulls. "Really? That's surprising. No wonder the pig didn't manage to kill you."

I laughed. "She'll probably try again. Now, what did you mean by my family knowing about Lloyd's misdeeds?"

Edna snapped the recliner upright, all the better to

stare me down with brown eyes that were still sharp. "Ask your sister."

"Which one? I have four. You vaccinated all of us."

"I did more than that," she said. "They were all pretty wild, except for you."

"Not Daisy," I said. "She was the model child and second mother to me."

"And now a mother to fools," Edna said. "What I wouldn't give to land a shot in the arms of those younger twins. Pranksters and brats."

I couldn't deny it, so I stuck to the point. "What does any of this have to do with Lloyd?"

"I have no idea." She leaned forward and stared at me. "But Daisy will. She was at your farm at four or five on Monday afternoon. Isn't that the time he supposedly died?"

My eyelids dropped instantly. I'd learned long ago that looking down bought a second or two to regain emotional mastery. But this took me so much by surprise that my lids actually locked in place. "She was at my place?"

"She didn't tell you? That seems strange, doesn't it? I assumed you knew."

Now my eyes met hers again. I hoped they were as hard and bright as I knew they could be when I was under siege. "My family is welcome to come and go as they like, of course. Daisy's been helping me with interior design for the inn. I expect she came to measure for the new rugs." I glanced around. "She has quite an eye, you know. If you're ever looking to refresh."

Edna's eyes were hard and bright, too. "This place

will look exactly as it does today when I'm carried out, feet first. But thank you."

"Well, it's lovely," I said, getting up and going to the window. "Just a little dim."

I started to pull back the curtains and she gave a loud squawk of protest. I soon saw why. On the window ledge sat a pair of binoculars. While Edna was still fighting her way out of the recliner, I held the binoculars to my eyes and directed them toward Runaway Farm.

"Give me those," she said, bustling over.

I stepped quickly to the right, fending her off with my left hand. "An unobstructed view, and the hill really helps. You've taken down a lot of trees to keep an eye on my place. Is that what they call being neighborly in Clover Grove these days?"

She yanked the binoculars out of my hand and I let them go so abruptly that she nearly stumbled. "A single senior can't be too careful," she said. "Your animals create havoc, and your sister's having liaisons with dubious characters in your own barn without your knowledge. Not to mention a murder in broad daylight. So yes, I'll keep an eye on your place, Ivy Galloway. Just so you know, I have a gun, too, and I'm trained to use it."

"You saw Lloyd *with* my sister?"

She shook her head, looking almost disappointed. "I saw her arrive and go in the house for a bit. Then Lloyd arrived on foot. He'd parked his truck out of sight somewhere. I guess Daisy saw him because she stormed out of the house and went down to the barn. She was probably giving him a piece of her mind over your fine."

"The fine I got because of you." I signaled Keats and then headed for the door.

"Now, don't be like that, Ivy. I'm just trying to keep this town safer for everybody. A dog that boldly chases chickens could just as easily attack children."

The heat that had never really left my face since the regifted pie revelation just burned a little brighter. "My dog would *never* attack children, Miss Evans, and I would thank you not to slander him."

She followed me to the door, chuckling. "You're an odd girl, Ivy. It seems like you're more indignant about my slandering your dog than your siblings."

With my hand on the doorknob, I turned and smiled. "Well, of course. My siblings can defend themselves—if there's anything to defend. Keats can't. And for your information, there's no better dog on the planet."

Rolling her eyes, she picked up the pie from the hall table. "Do you want to pawn Gwen's pie off on someone who likes peaches?"

"All yours. I'm sure the pastry is delicious." I opened the door and added, "You never know who might be arriving hungry."

Closing the door quickly, I hurried down the front walk and met Kellan halfway.

"How'd the apology go?" he asked.

"Great," I said, rolling my eyes. "Aside from Edna dissing my regifted pie, we bonded like only good neighbours can."

"You regifted?" His teeth flashed in a rare smile. "That's a fineable offence under town pielaws."

I laughed, despite the anxiety sitting like a fat pig on

my chest. He was obviously going inside to interview Edna about what she saw on the day of Lloyd's murder and she'd waste no time implicating Daisy. The only thing worse than being accused myself was seeing my sister in trouble. On the bright side, Edna would undoubtedly drag out her moment of glory, which meant I should be able to reach Daisy first.

"I came here to grovel, Kellan," I said. "What's your excuse?"

He shrugged. "Just a chat. When someone dies, you chat with all the neighbours. Routine police work."

"Why don't you chat to people with a motive to kill Lloyd first?" I asked. "Like Nadine or the people who shot at him?"

My tone was edgier than I intended and his eyebrows went up. "I don't need advice on how to do my job, Ivy."

"Sorry," I said, slipping past him. "Grovelling makes me grumpy. Especially after getting rolled by a pig."

"If it helps, you smell much better," he said.

"Gee thanks," I said, opening the door of the truck.

Keats jumped in and I was about to follow when Kellan called after me. "Ivy?"

"Yeah?"

"You're staying out of this like I asked, right?"

"It's only been two hours, Chief," I called back. "And it's not like I don't have my hands full enough. My first guests arrive in less than three weeks and everything needs to be perfect. If you could clear my farm's name by then, I'll give you all the free pie you could ever want."

"Doing my best," he said. "Behave or I'll assign a police detail, and they won't be as nice as Asher."

Giving him a wave, I climbed into the driver's seat. I fussed with my purse, hoping Kellan would go inside. Instead he stood on the bottom step watching until I finally turned the key in the ignition. Putting the truck in reverse, I stalled out immediately. With my face nearly in flames, I did it again. And again. Why did driving backwards seem so much harder with a stick? And an audience?

By the time I managed to turn the truck around, Kellan was grinning from ear to ear. I'd forgotten how gorgeous his smile was, and it was a shame I wasn't likely to see it again anytime soon.

On an up note, I managed to burn some rubber on Edna's short driveway as I pounded the gas and screeched away. In the country, the first time you lay a patch is a rite of passage.

It was never too late to come of age.

CHAPTER TWELVE

I stalled another six times, maybe more, on the way to Daisy's house. So many that Keats crawled between the seats to sit in the rear on the floor. "I'm sorry buddy, really. I'm just freaking out a bit right now." I dared to take a quick glance and saw one blue eye looking up at me reproachfully. "Well, come on. Edna all but said Daisy murdered Lloyd. You know Daisy. She's the last person in Clover Grove who'd ever kill someone." I thought about that and added, "Unless she was defending her family. If a space alien came down and tried to abduct any of us, she'd slay it, for sure."

I took a deep breath and focused as I made the last turn. The left turns scared me the most. What if I stalled in oncoming traffic? With my stick skills declining rapidly, it was a real risk.

The younger twins, now 14, were shooting hoops in the driveway when I pulled in. They nearly collapsed in joint hilarity when I not only stalled the truck but started rolling back down the small incline. I managed to pull the parking brake in time and they ran down to greet me. Reese had done me the favor of getting a tattoo of a treble clef on his ear so that I could finally tell them apart. He said it was because of the girls. He was a natural flirt, but Beaton was always swooping in for the close after Reese had done the hard work. Both boys were in a rock band of questionable talent and were never short of female admirers.

I held the phone to my ear and signalled I'd join them in a second. In truth, I just wanted a chance to collect my thoughts before confronting Daisy. But when the boys resumed their game of one-on one, something struck me for the first time. They were cute boys who would soon be handsome men... and they didn't look one bit like their dad, Roger. The older twins, on the other hand, were the spitting image of their dad, with brown, curly hair and dark eyes. Beaton and Reese, however, had blue eyes and russet hair verging on auburn.

Reaching into my purse, I touched the framed photo I'd taken from Lloyd's bedroom. Was it possible?

"You look sick," Reese said, when I finally got out of the truck. My legs felt wobbly and my stomach percolated like a geyser.

"'Sick' is good, right?" I said. "That's what you told me last year."

"Just don't, Aunt Ivy. Trying too hard to be cool is pathetic."

"I know," I admitted. "I'm not myself today. I got rolled by a pig earlier."

The boys didn't even pretend to feel bad. They leaned against the garage door howling with laughter as I shared the details. I knew it would solidify my reputation as the "fun" aunt. Unlike my older sisters, I was never hard on the boys, even though they got into trouble on the regular. It hadn't bothered me because I'd never lived under the shadow of their escapades.

The short interlude gave me a chance to get my game face on before I went in to speak to Daisy. "Give us a few minutes alone, would you?" I said. "I have a personal problem I want to talk to your mom about."

"I heard you've got it bad for the police chief," Reese said. "Uncle Ash told us you were staring at him all flirty and trying to get him to eat your pie. At a crime scene."

"He what? Oh my god. I'll kill— You know what? Never mind."

"Don't try so hard," one of them called after me. "It's pathetic."

I stalked away, blocking them all out of my mind. Compartmentalize, I told myself. It was normally one of my stronger skills. Right now, my main goal was warning Daisy.

She was scrubbing the kitchen counter when I walked in, which was business as usual. Daisy wasn't a full-on germophobe, but close enough that living with five males was probably torture. At home, there was rarely a time she didn't have spray cleaner in one hand and a cloth in the other.

"Hey Ivy," she said, eyes dropping to the counter as she resumed her thankless job. "What brings you here?"

"The fact that you haven't come to me," I said. "You rush to my side when there's a curtain and carpet crisis but not when a body's been found on my property?"

Her hazel eyes flicked up at me and there was a strange look in her eyes. If I didn't know my sensible, cheery sister better, I'd say she looked haunted. "I did drop by and saw you were in capable hands with Jilly," she said. "I've had my hands full the past two days and I knew Asher had you covered, too."

I leaned against the counter and crossed my arms. "What's up? It's not like you to let me manage my own crisis. And you certainly wouldn't trust Ash to cover my butt." I stooped to catch her eye. "Unless you were busy covering your own."

"Cover my butt? What do you mean?" Her calm voice spiked in a way I'd never heard before. "What have I got to hide?"

"Good question. Let's start with the basics. What were you doing at Runaway Farm on the afternoon Lloyd died? My nosy neighbor Edna places you there sometime between four and five p.m."

"Edna Evans? The sadistic nurse?" Daisy almost spit the words. "She spies on you?"

"With binoculars. She saw you go into the house, and then charge out a little later and run down to the barn. Not long after Lloyd had apparently arrived on foot. According to her, you were liaising with Lloyd in the barn and came out alone."

"I was not liaising with Lloyd Boyce on Monday afternoon." She spritzed a new coating of spray on the counter. "I went to measure for the rugs. Then I saw Lloyd poking around where he didn't belong and went down to speak to him about the fine he gave you that morning."

"And how did that go?"

Slamming the spray bottle down, she glared at me. "What is this? The Spanish Inquisition?"

"It's a dress rehearsal," I said, without flinching. She used to intimidate me but not so much anymore. "Because Chief Harper will probably be here shortly. He was going in to speak to Edna as I came out. She'll share the same story."

"Oh no. But the boys..." She shoved her hair back with one rubber-gloved hand. "I don't want them to know."

Another thing I'd learned in HR was to rip the Band-Aid off the truth quickly and get an honest reaction before people slid into a rehearsed script. If the secret was big enough—and this was a huge one—people always had a script. "About Lloyd being their dad?" I asked.

The rubber glove moved to Daisy's throat, as if she were choking. The strangled words that came out confirmed it. "How did you—?"

I pulled the photo out of my purse and handed it to her. "This was on Lloyd's dresser. I started putting the pieces together and came up with the theory you've just confirmed. The blue eyes, the auburn hair. They don't look like Roger. My guess is that Lloyd consoled you during the period you and Roger separated. The math works out right."

She literally sank to the floor, sliding down the smooth wood of the cupboards and covering her face with the rubber gloves. "Ivy. Please don't tell Roger or the kids. I'm so ashamed."

"Roger doesn't know?" I asked. "How could he not wonder?"

"He doesn't like to think about the time he walked out on us. He's ashamed, too, and he's blocked out the memory. So I guess he hasn't looked too closely. We got together again so fast that the boys could have been his. I wasn't sure myself when they were babies."

I sat down on the floor too and Keats stretched out beside me. His ears were pricked and his eyes alert, as if to take in every word and gesture. "Daisy, it's okay. We all have our moments. I've certainly had my share and I'm not one to judge. What I'm worried about now is the police. You went down to my barn to confront Lloyd. Was it really about the ticket?"

Her face was still covered with rubber gloves. "No. Lloyd figured things out about the boys three years ago and wanted to get to know them. I refused. They were so young and always getting into trouble." The gloves came down. "Lloyd's genes, obviously. Roger never—"

"Focus," I said. "We don't have much time and you need to get your story straight."

"There's no story. Lloyd had texted me again and when I saw him go into the barn I went down there. We argued about it. I probably yelled."

"Were there any witnesses? I mean, nearby?"

"Only the horse," she said. "I told him in no uncertain terms to back off. That the boys were at a tricky age and I had to get them through high school in one piece. He said it wasn't fair—that I was just trying to protect my marriage." She started pushing back up the cupboards, and I got to my feet, too. "Can you blame me? This is my family."

"I know you'd throw yourself in front of a train for those boys. You're a mama bear and a force of nature. But you wouldn't..."

My voice trailed off and she continued for me. "Kill Lloyd? Of course not, Ivy. Even if I *could* strangle him, like Asher said happened, I wouldn't. He was still the boys' father and I intended to tell them someday." Her wild eyes calmed somewhat. "Truly. All I did was yell some common sense into him and then I left in a big huff. He followed me out still trying to convince me, and I assumed he left, too. I told him to get off your property or I'd call the cops, but he knew I wouldn't."

I waited a few beats and then asked, "That was it?"

She nodded. "I felt so embarrassed and guilty I didn't want to tell anyone. I thought I was in the clear, since no one had seen me."

"Okay. Okay." I ran my hands through my hair. "I already texted Asher. He should be here soon and can run interference."

"No! I don't want him to know any of this."

"But then you'll have to go in for questioning alone."

"I'm sure the chief has to keep my secret about Lloyd's role in my past."

"But people will talk anyway when you become a suspect. They'll put you under the Clover Grove micro-scope and maybe someone will figure it out. If I could see the resemblance, others might, too."

"Don't say that." She started scrubbing the counter anew. "It could really confuse the boys, and you know they've had some challenges." Finally she turned. "What should I do?"

It was a momentous day—the first time my capable older sister ever asked *me* for advice. What a shame it had to be a really tough question that I didn't know how to answer.

"Daisy, you're just going to have to tell Kellan the truth, and ask him to keep the personal aspect quiet, given that the boys are minors. If he doesn't agree, you'll have to tell Asher, too, and read him the riot act. It's not as if he doesn't have plenty of skeletons in his own closet." I straightened my shoulders and smiled. "If it comes down to sibling blackmail, I'll back you."

"But what do I say about what happened with Lloyd? It sounds like I was the last to see him alive."

"Not the last," I said. "I just have to figure out who the last person really was."

"You? I hope you mean the police, Ivy. You shouldn't be putting yourself in harm's way." Now my older sister was back. I could see it in the way she rose to her full height again. The gloves came off and slapped onto the counter and she put her bare hands on her hips. "On that note, how did you happen to be in Lloyd's bedroom to find this photo?"

"I was there to feed his reptile collection, at Nadine's request," I said. "Long story. And a good one, when we have more time."

"His reptile collection? How many are there?"

"Lots. Three exotic constrictors, one of them huge. I bet the boys would love to get their hands on *that* inheritance."

It wasn't often that my sister's ruddy complexion paled, but it did now. "You must never ever mention those illegal snakes to the boys. They've always had a fascination for reptiles beyond what's normal. Now I know why."

"Trust me, I have no desire to see them again."

She pulled an elastic out of her pocket and put her hair in a smooth ponytail. "Whatever happens next, I know I made the right decision in keeping the boys away from Lloyd."

I nodded. "Nurture over nature. You and Roger are going to make good men of them yet."

"All I have to do is put the murder accusations behind me and I can go back to being the perfect mom."

"That's the spirit," I said, smiling.

She reached out and gripped my hand tightly. "But if anything goes wrong, Ivy, please promise you'll help Roger raise the boys. You have more common sense than the rest of the family put together."

My heart filled with a mixture of pride and fear. "Daisy, don't you dare leave me to raise those hooligans. Get yourself together and fight this like the mama bear you are."

"It gets so tiring, you know," she said, straightening as the doorbell rang. "Maybe prison would be a nice vacation."

CHAPTER THIRTEEN

M y scream startled Florence so much that she reared in her stall and echoed the sound.

"For pity's sake, would you ladies keep it down?" Charlie asked.

I ran to his side and fell to my knees. "I thought you were dead, Charlie."

"I'm still on the right side of the grass, though a little worse for wear." He was lying flat on his back inside the pen with the goats. We never left them out overnight, even with their fierce donkey guardians.

"Keats, keep them back," I said, gesturing to the livestock. The dog slipped past me and pinned the goats in the corner. "Is it your heart, Charlie?"

He shook his head. "My knee. Nothing serious, so don't worry your pretty head. Still, I'm going to need a hand to get to my truck."

"What happened?" I pulled him into a sitting position and stared around.

"Twine across the doorway into the pen. Oldest trick

in the book. And I fell for it." He forced a grin. "Literally. I cut it so you didn't trip, too."

"You're saying someone rigged up a trap for you?"

"Or you. But yeah, someone wanted one of us out of commission."

"But why?"

"Can we debate this when I'm on my feet? There's nothing more humiliating for an old farmhand than being flat out in manure."

I looked around for something to help him up. He was a tall, sturdy man and I risked injuring him further by doing the job wrong. I thought about getting Jilly out of bed to help but that was only going to damage Charlie's pride further. Besides, problem solving was part of a farm-owner's skill set.

My sheep hook! That was just the thing. I stood and turned so quickly my head spun... and what I saw didn't help. The place on the wall where my red and white sheep hook normally hung was bare. I hadn't used it since before I'd decided to move to Runaway Farm. One day I might join herding trials again because Keats had loved our hobby. But it wouldn't be till the inn was up and running smoothly.

"What's wrong?" Charlie asked, blue eyes squinting up at me.

"Nothing. Just looking for the pig poker. I think it's out near Wilma." I ran to the back door. "Hang tight."

"I'm not going anywhere," he called after me.

The heavy wood poker did the trick, and he was soon up and going, using the pole as a cane. "Are you sure you're good to drive?" I asked as he maneuvered himself into his truck. "I'd rather take you to the clinic myself."

"God gave me two legs for a reason," he said, smiling down from the driver's seat. "I'd have to be pushing up daisies before I let you bunny-hop me into town."

"Very funny." It did make me smile, though. "Charlie, why is someone sabotaging us? First they let Wilma out and now they rigged a trap that could have given one of us a concussion. Banging up my brain again would not bode well for Runaway Farm."

Turning the key, he raised his voice over the motor. "Honestly, Ivy, I think it's time you involved the police. Not your brother. Real police."

"They are involved. And Asher is real police."

Charlie rolled his eyes. "I've known that boy since he was knee-high and he'll never be a real cop. Too soft."

"Well, I did tell Chief Harper about someone vandalizing the pig pen."

"Yeah, but you're not telling him everything. I can tell. And I can tell you don't trust him." I started to protest and Charlie pressed on. "If I had to hazard a guess, I'd say you two had a thing once and someone isn't over it yet."

My face twitched as if I'd been hit by a cattle prod and frustration followed. I used to have the blandest face in every room. A blank slate. That gave me a certain power. Of all the harm my accident caused, losing complete emotional mastery was probably the worst.

"That was a long time ago," I said, closing the driver's door. "So long ago it doesn't matter."

He rolled down the window. "Not so long that it isn't

obvious to anyone with horse sense. Normally my advice is to just let things unfold naturally. In this case, however, I think you're going to need to suck it up and apologize to the man so that you can get the protection you need."

I crossed my arms. "What makes you think I'm the one who needs to apologize?"

He pressed his good foot to the pedal, making the motor roar. "I know a man who's been hurt when I see one." Before I could respond, he put the truck in gear and started rolling slowly. "Because I see the same look in my own mirror every day."

"Charlie!" I called after him.

His hand came out in a wave and then he gunned the truck down the curving driveway.

SNEAKING into Lloyd's house in broad daylight was terrifying in a whole different way. Now I was worried about being spotted by someone who'd call the police. But at least I'd be able to see the snakes coming.

"I'm not going down there. Don't worry," I told Keats as we pushed through the bushes to the side door. "They can live on what I gave them until Nadine takes care of it or Kellan takes over. Today, we're going to focus, Keats. No distractions like family secrets or exotic reptiles. We're here to find out what that key opens. If I'm right, it'll take us to the murderer."

Keats gave an anxious whine as I pulled on rubber gloves before opening the back door. It wasn't a warning, just a complaint. He wasn't one to back down from adventure. Far from it. More likely he was picking up on my worries.

"It's okay, buddy. I'm not scared. Or at least, not any more scared than someone heading into a snake pit would normally feel." I hurried up the stairs and down the hall to Lloyd's bedroom with a quick glance around to make sure I was alone. "I'm just thinking about what Charlie said, and I'm afraid he's right. I can't go all maverick on this just because I'm uncomfortable with Kellan. Now that Charlie's been hurt, I need to share everything."

Keats turned his brown eye in my direction—the benevolent eye that offered canine approval.

There was no time to muse on high school heart-break, however. Lloyd's room was dark because his heavy curtains were still closed. I flipped on my phone light and pulled the key I snatched from the snake tank out of my pocket. It looked too big to fit in the lock of the big wooden trunk, and I was right. That left the closet. The key slipped easily into the lock and I looked down at Keats. "I lied before," I said. "I am scared."

He might as well have nodded. I knew he knew. There was never any point in trying to hide my feelings from this dog.

"Anything could be behind this door. Another secret room. Dangerous animals." I took a deep breath. "Even a body. Do you smell anything?"

Keats gave a single swish of his tail that reassured me. No way would he swish if there were dangerous animals or bodies inside.

I twisted the knob and opened, expecting the worst. But one flash of my light made me laugh out loud.

"Toys, Keats. Toys!"

Neatly arranged on shelves were boxed collectibles and comic books in plastic sleeves. I took a closer look and recognized more than a few of the superhero faces.

"These are worth a bundle," I said, snapping photos. "And maybe they're even worth killing someone over, to another crazed collector."

Locking the door again, I led Keats back through the house to the side door. The dog made little squeaking noises that seemed to be urging me on. I locked the exterior door, too, and then turned and bent over the Buddha statue to replace the key. I didn't intend to come back again.

"Say a prayer while you're down there," someone said.

I froze, my butt directed at the speaker. Luckily, he'd admired that butt once. Hopefully it was still a pleasant distraction.

"Oh, hi Kellan," I said, standing. "How are you?"

He tipped his head to one side. "How about we save the pleasantries till after you tell me why you broke into Lloyd Boyce's house. I'm too curious to wait."

I gave him a good smile—one that was not quite genuine but not super fake either. Did other people have a smile ranking system like mine?

"It's not breaking in if you have a key," I said, peeling off the rubber gloves.

"Yeah, Ivy, it is," he said. "And it's mighty suspicious behavior when the owner in question happened to die on your property a few days ago."

"The previous co-owner gave me permission. In fact, Nadine *asked* me to come by and feed Lloyd's pets."

"What pets?"

I came down the stairs to join him. Keats sat by my feet and wrapped his tail neatly around his paws. "Assorted reptiles, if you call them pets. I don't. Oh, and the tarantula, too."

Kellan stared at me, possibly wondering if I was joking. "I've been through the house twice and all I've seen is a cage of mice in the living room."

"Food for the serpents. Luckily they'll eat frozen too, because there was no way I would offer live mice."

"Where are they?"

"There are two albino Burmese pythons and another snake downstairs in a secret room. Plus a big lizard and the aforementioned tarantula, among other things. I'll leave their care and feeding to you after this, if you don't mind."

"Well, that explains the mice in the freezer," he said. "I assumed he was taking them in to animal services."

"More like he was bringing confiscated reptiles home from animal services. I'm sure Nadine will tell you about how that helped to drive them apart."

He stared at me. "She hasn't mentioned that in either of our conversations."

"She wanted to take care of this herself. It would make her look bad for turning a blind eye to this, she said, and damage her business. Not to mention lowering the value of the house." I sighed. "I felt bad for her, because she was even more terrified of the snakes than I was."

He rubbed his face with both hands. "I can't believe

you, Ivy. You went into a secret snake room without telling the police. Who knows what could have happened?"

"Well, one of them could certainly have squeezed the life out of me."

"You, as well as other members of the community, if you'd made a mistake. Children. Pets. Did you think about that?"

I sat down hard on the stairs. "Actually, no. But I was super careful, and nothing happened."

He paced back and forth, obviously trying to hold in his frustration. "I realize how much is riding on this for you, but this isn't your private mission and you can't be so reckless."

Shame kept my eyes on the ground. "You're right, that was stupid. I think she might have played me."

"I don't know about that, but I do know that you should have called me. I'll get experienced snake handlers to deal with this today."

"Well, I hope she's not mad at me for telling you now. Because if she murdered Lloyd, she might come after me."

"Her alibi checked out," he said. "Hot yoga class. Another stupid fad that's come to Clover Grove."

"Yeah? Well, I still think it might be her. She had a lot to gain." I gestured to the house. "Once the snakes are gone, this will be worth a ton."

"They seemed to be on good terms, all things considered. I don't know yet if she was aware of his affair with your sister, though. Perhaps that added some tension."

My face practically detonated. Hearing it said out

loud and so casually made me furious. This could tatter Daisy's stellar reputation and hurt the boys.

"That was long before Nadine's time with Lloyd," I said. "He was single and Daisy was separated, too. Stupid flings happen all the time."

"Yeah. I guess they do," he said.

There was a distinct edge of bitterness in his voice—enough that Keats got to his feet. Maybe the dog was signalling that it was time. Either time to go, or time to confront the demons of our past. I stood up, too, and straightened my shoulders.

"Kellan. If you are in any way comparing this to our relationship in high school, let's set the record straight. I know what people said. I know they thought I was cheating on you. And it was never true." My voice quavered and Keats leaned into my leg. "I still can't believe you actually bought into those rumours. You knew me better than that."

He turned to face the front of the house. "I don't want to talk about the old days, Ivy. I'm here to solve a murder, and I know you want that done, too. So you might as well tell me what you know right now. Save me the effort of calling you in daily for questioning."

I backed up and sat down on the stairs and Keats did the same. Kellan shook his head and nearly smiled.

"Before I tell you, I need to know you've ruled Daisy out as a suspect."

"You don't get to set conditions. I took your brother off the case to shut down the information pipeline. Asher's a good man but he can't keep his lips sealed."

"He's the white sheep of the family," I said. "Obviously Daisy and I know how to keep a secret." I crossed my arms and smiled. "I suppose you could torture it out of me if you like."

He shook his head. "We're not in the business of torture in Clover Grove. But since you're as stubborn as ever, I will tell you that I don't believe Daisy killed Lloyd. Unfortunately, I have Edna's statement and Daisy's confirmation that she was in the wrong place at the right time. So she's still on the list of possibilities, unless you have better ideas for me. Sharing them will help me clear your sister's name."

Picking up a stick, I started tracing lines in the sandy soil at the base of the steps. "There's a locked closet full of toys in Lloyd's bedroom."

"Toys? What kind of toys?"

"Collectibles. The expensive type, if I've learned anything from Asher's interest over the years." I reached into my pocket and then offered him the key. "This was in the tank with the biggest python. I distracted her with a mouse and grabbed it."

Eyebrows rising, he said, "Seriously? You're that nosy?"

"That stupid, I guess. But the stakes are high, Kellan. I could lose the farm. It's not just a saying anymore. I poured all the savings I had into this and no one is going to want to vacation there with an unsolved murder hanging over it." I scratched a big X into the earth. "Maybe even after it's solved, since someone is sabotaging me."

"What else has happened?" His voice was sharp now.

"First someone set Wilma loose, as you know. And

today someone set a rope snare in one of the pens and tripped Charlie. He hurt his knee and is off duty till further notice." I looked up at him. "I assume that was intended for me, and someone wants me out of business."

The hard look in his eyes softened. "Ivy, you've got to be careful."

"I know. Because that's not all. I think I know the murder weapon, too."

I told him about the missing sheep hook and he took notes, frowning the entire time. "It fits with the autopsy report," he said. "There was bruising around the neck along with ligature marks from something else. Just to add complexity, there was poison in Lloyd's system."

"Poison?"

"Rat poison. Not enough to kill him but enough to disable him, perhaps, so that he could be more easily killed."

Maybe a bellyful of rat poison was the reason Lloyd had looked so haggard when he gave me the ticket the day he died. I thought he'd just aged prematurely from the stress of seizing people's dogs.

I got to my feet and gestured to Keats. "You checked the baked goods in Lloyd's fridge? I saw them when I was collecting the mice."

"Getting them tested, yes." He followed me to the edge of the bush. "Stay out of this, Ivy. The farm won't be much good to you if you're injured."

"I've faced worse before," I said, resting my hand on Keats' head. "Some things are worth fighting for and I don't intend to stop now."

"If I have to, I'll—"

"Find a reason to arrest me. I know. But I've just given you a couple of solid leads, Kellan. Find the collectors of exotic pets and superhero toys."

He was still protesting as I pushed into the bushes, and I called back, "You're wasting time, Chief. Go get your man."

CHAPTER FOURTEEN

I'd had no trouble finding Nadine's house because Charlie told me about the ornate sign on the front lawn advertising her services as a realtor. He was now home and comfortable after getting an X-ray. Nothing but torn ligaments, apparently, but he'd still be off for a couple of weeks. Luckily I still had Gwen Quinn's card, and she gladly agreed to step in as farmhand. She didn't seem fazed by the recent "pranks" at the farm, noting that plenty of people were still bitter about things that had happened at Runaway Farm before my time. She promised to double check everything morning and night. That made me feel a little calmer as I walked up Nadine's front stairs.

Nadine's finely-plucked eyebrows rose when she opened the door and saw me on the porch with Keats. "Ivy, what a surprise. Come in, both of you."

I could tell at a glance there'd be no offer of baked goods here. Nadine was in a scanty yoga outfit and there wasn't an ounce of pie on her. Clearly there was a lot to be said for so-called fads like hot yoga.

"I won't keep you long," I said, following her into the living room and taking a seat on the couch. "I just wanted to chat about the farm with you. I think you may have been right."

"How so?" She sank gracefully into a chair and crossed her legs, lotus style.

I scratched Keats' head, considering my wording. "So many things have gone wrong lately that I'm starting to think it really is cursed. I'm afraid of what's coming next." I sat back and sighed. "On top of that, I'm afraid I'm going to lose my shirt because the inn won't succeed. Maybe I was better off in the city."

"Don't be so hasty," she said. "It's far too early to give up on Clover Grove." Her voice was rich and soothing... almost seductive. "The police will get this sorted out soon enough and you'll get your inn launched. I really think there's a market for the upscale farm experience."

"I don't know. I'm just getting a really bad feeling about it. You predicted I'd want to sell and I guess you were right."

Her eyes widened and I wondered how she kept her makeup so nice if hot yoga was her passion.

"I'm so sorry I discouraged you, Ivy. This is your dream and you need to give it a fair try. I shouldn't have been so flippant."

"You were just being honest and I appreciate it. I didn't want to believe the place had a black cloud over it. First, Lloyd, and now someone is sabotaging my animals." I told her briefly about the rogue pig and Charlie's accident. "I'm so stressed about everything that I think I need to bail while I still can."

Nadine unfolded her elegant legs and came over to perch beside me on the couch. "Ivy, just relax. I have complete faith in Chief Harper. He'll get to the bottom of this soon. Lloyd didn't cover all his tracks, I'm quite sure of that."

"I can't relax. What if Lloyd was just in the wrong place at the wrong time? Maybe someone was actually trying to kill *me* and he got in the way?"

"I doubt that very much." She patted my leg with a perfectly manicured hand. "You haven't been around long enough to have enemies like Lloyd did. Now, take a deep breath. *In for five, out for five. In for five, out for five.*"

I did as she said and felt calmer instantly. "Maybe I should try yoga. What's the best studio in town? I was surprised to see so many had cropped up."

"Serenity Yoga Studio, hands down. Try the hot class with Hayden. It'll change your life." Getting up, she walked over to the doorway to the kitchen. There was a chin-up bar mounted near the top. Wrapping her fingers around it, she knocked off a few lifts with impressive ease. "Before Hayden I could barely lift a coffee mug," she said, dropping to the floor.

"Wow. Sold. I'll definitely give it a try." Blowing out another deep breath, I said, "Would you mind if I had a glass of water? I think all the stress is dehydrating me."

I followed her into the kitchen, peering around as she opened the fridge and reached for a bottle of water. In the corner near the back door sat the box I'd seen in her basket at Myrtle's the day we'd met. Rat poison.

She offered me the water. "Drink up. And then proceed directly to yoga. If you still want to think about selling the farm in a few months, I'm your gal."

"But I want to sell right now, before I lose my investment." I twisted open the bottle of water and took a swig. "This took everything I had, Nadine."

Looking down at Keats, she leaned against the counter and sighed. "Honey, I've got to be honest. You won't get your investment back today—not with a murder hanging over the farm. Even developers shy away from things like that. And unless my intel is wrong, there are stipulations on your selling to developers anyway. Hannah Pemberton was adamant about keeping her animals safe."

"Your intel is correct." I paced up and down the ivory tile floor. "I'd need to speak to her first, of course. She couldn't have envisioned someone being killed at Runaway Farm or Charlie being injured. Her animals aren't safe now as it is, let alone me and my staff and friends."

"I'm sure you're exaggerating the risk." It looked like she was trying to frown but the muscles of her face didn't move much. Botox, perhaps. "Just give things time to settle."

"I don't have time, and I don't have as much faith in the police as you do." I stared at her earnestly. "Can you think of anything I could look into? Any other enemies Lloyd might have?"

"Honestly, he had plenty. It seemed like he was

always in trouble with someone." She pushed her hair back and sighed. "He came to me for money not long ago. As if I'd give him a cent when he was stalling on finalizing the divorce settlement. Like I told you before, he was worried about the reptiles. Where would he put them if he had to downgrade to an apartment?"

"I'm sure you just wanted it over and behind you."

"You can't imagine how much." She gestured around the small house. "I'm only renting here because I couldn't sell our joint property. But I tried to be patient. A good person." She pushed off the counter and got a bottle of water from the fridge herself. "The snakes mattered to him more than I did."

"I doubt that's true. He seemed disheartened over the divorce the day we spoke."

She chugged half the water and wiped her mouth on her bare arm. "Not enough to part with his prize pythons. The biggest one could have easily killed him. Or me, if she got out. I lived in fear."

"He must have liked the thrill," I said. "She was terrifying."

"I haven't thanked you properly," she said, squeezing my arm. "You're very brave."

"You'll tell the chief, though, right? I don't think I can face it again."

"I'll tell him everything," she said. "We're meeting again later and I doubt he'll be as easy on me this time."

"You have nothing to hide," I said. "The more you share, the sooner this is all over and you move on."

"I've been wracking my brains trying to come up with

names for him. But Lloyd didn't really confide in me anymore. Understandably."

"Why would he be short of money? He had a civic job that probably paid decently."

"He always had expensive hobbies," she said. "When I didn't offer him money, he said there were places in town he could get it. I'm seriously hoping he didn't do anything stupid, because they could come after me to recover the debt."

"Like a loan shark? Or a gang?"

She shrugged. "I only hear rumours. And seriously, Ivy, you do not want to go nosing around in that dirty business. Clover Grove has a dark side, too."

"Really?" Now my surprise was genuine. "I had no idea."

"Sorry to disillusion you. Mostly it's as bucolic as the marketing material says." She gestured toward the front door. "I hate to rush you, but I've got a house showing in half an hour and need to put on something more sedate." She grinned at me. "Yoga still gets a bad rap from the old schoolers. Clover Grove is stuck in a time warp."

I took a detour to the back door and picked up the box of rat poison. It was light—nearly empty. "This stuff work?" I asked. "I've had a heck of a time with rats at the farm. Hannah's dog was a ratter but it's beneath Keats, I'm afraid."

She nodded. "It's done the job here, although it's taken a couple of boxes. I wouldn't recommend it on the farm though. What if one of your critters ate a poisoned rat? I actually had Lloyd come by and deal with the remains." She waved an elegant hand. "No way was I touching them."

I stopped at the front door. "Thanks for your advice, Nadine. Please keep me posted if you hear of anyone who might be interested in buying a cursed farm."

"Oh, stop it. That is the last time I ever joke like that with potential clients. I could get a bad reputation myself." She shrugged. "Worse than being a potential murderer, that is."

I tipped my head. "You're taking it pretty well."

"Yoga," she said, with a beatific smile. "I've surrendered to the process, and you should, too. The truth will come out and we'll get on with our lives." She looked down at Keats and he stared up at her. "You too, handsome."

Keats' tail rose and gave a restrained wave. Normally he was immune to flattery but he seemed rather disposed to Nadine. The yoga wear was wasted on him but he did like a seductive voice.

I doubted he was alone in that, and I was determined to find out.

CHAPTER FIFTEEN

Gwen was hurling hay bales around with ease when I went down to the barn the next morning after another four-course breakfast in Jilly's test kitchen. Since moving here I'd adopted intermittent fasting without meaning to. One day I feasted, the next I fasted unintentionally while I chased pigs or clues. The result was some weight loss I hadn't really needed. On the bright side, I wouldn't look half bad in Jilly's borrowed yoga gear when we joined Hayden for yoga later.

"I just wanted to thank you again for pitching in for Charlie. Literally," I said when Gwen turned. "You're a lifesaver."

"Not at all," she said, pushing back her Clover Grove Herding Club cap with the little black sheep on the logo. "This is my idea of play, not work. Maybe I could borrow Keats later to chase the sheep around. I want to practice my moves before the herding trial next week."

Keats eased behind me as if he'd understood her

words. "He's coming with me today," I said. "Like every day, pretty much. We've been tied at the hip since I rescued him."

Gwen looked down and saw the dog lurking behind me and laughed. "Mama's boy. Maybe I'll swing home and get Paisley if you don't mind another dog on the property."

"Not at all. Keats isn't territorial. And the sheep are all yours."

Gwen peered around. "Where's your sheep hook? I could have used it yesterday. One of the ewes got flighty."

My eyes shot to the wall where it had hung, hoping it might have suddenly materialized. "Lost track of it after I moved," I said, improvising on the fly. "It'll turn up eventually."

"It better," Gwen said. "Around here they say much depends on your lucky hook."

"Well, that explains a lot, I guess." I gave Florence a kiss on her graying muzzle. "I haven't had much luck since I got here, and unless it turns, my inn's doomed."

"Never mind that kind of talk," Gwen said, going back to forking hay into the cow pen. "I'll look around for it today while I'm playing with the sheep."

"Sounds good," I said, heading back to where Jilly was waiting by the truck. She didn't go into the barn unless she absolutely had to. Her clothes, shoes and hair still said city girl and I doubted that would change, no matter how long she stayed.

"Is it my imagination or is your driving getting worse instead of better?" she asked, bracing herself on the dash as I lurched down the long lane.

Keats gave a little whine from the small rear seat, possibly agreeing. He was also out of sorts about being ousted by Jilly from the passenger seat.

"You may be right," I said, turning onto the highway. "Nerves, I guess."

"And focus, or lack thereof. Seems like your mind is a hundred places at once."

"Make that two hundred. On top of the work for the inn, I'm constantly looking for new clues to Lloyd's murder. Not to mention worrying about the current family drama."

She gave me a sideways glance. "Did Daisy tell Asher about what happened?"

Daisy's dalliance with Lloyd was a delicate topic but I'd confided in Jilly anyway, knowing I could trust her never to spill. She was a professional keeper of secrets, just as I'd been. We offered that outlet to each other.

"About running into Lloyd in the barn, yes. Their old affair is staying a secret, aside from you and Chief Harper."

"That's going to be hard. You sisters are... well, like sisters."

I laughed. "Sounds about right. We're all as different as the flowers Mom named us after." I managed to negotiate a couple of long curves and two stoplights without stalling. "I guess we all have secrets. Maybe it's just a matter of time before they come spilling out."

"The upside of being an only child," she said as I turned into the parking lot at Myrtle's Store, "is that the only secrets are mine and no one cares."

"Oh, I don't know about that." I turned off the truck

and grinned at her. "How about the time you and that mechanic—"

"Nothing I've done measures up to you taking a baseball bat to—"

"Let's leave our secrets in the truck," I said, hopping out and releasing Keats. "Stick with the plan today, okay? No freestyling."

"Got it." She followed me inside and took a seat at the long counter beside the Hodgsons and their crossword puzzle. Before I'd reached the cash register, she was deep in conversation about the weather, a topic of endless interest in Clover Grove.

Myrtle looked up from her laptop with a smile. "Hi hon. Good to see you. Coffee and treat of the day?"

"Coffee, yes, times two. To go, please. I'll skip the treats." The plate of blueberry squares actually made my stomach turn, and it wasn't just from the big breakfast. I couldn't help thinking about the one in Lloyd's fridge and wondering if it had been spiked with poison. If so, Mandy was another suspect, but Nadine had plenty of opportunity, too. She could have thanked Lloyd for his dead rat disposal with a nice selection of baked goods.

"How about some oatmeal to go instead? It's gotten popular lately, thanks to Mandy's secret flavor packet." Myrtle grinned at me. "She's on a mission to promote regularity throughout Wolff County."

"A worthy cause, but Jilly's vegan test recipes have me covered."

"So you're holding up okay?" she asked, as she poured coffee into two paper cups. "Terrible shame you've had to deal with all of this so soon after coming home. I got an email from your mom and she's beside herself."

"I bet she is. I've been avoiding her calls, to be honest. But I'll have to see her at Asher's birthday party when she gets back. Which reminds me... I need to get him a gift. Any idea where I could get my hands on an original Wonder Woman collectible doll? He's wanted it forever and I feel bad about him being reassigned to highway patrol because of me. Now's the time to come through with the toys, but I've left it pretty late."

Myrtle gave me her sharp-eyed stare and I returned it with my blandest smile.

"I might know someone," she said. "Although he apparently hates parting with anything."

"I'll make it worth his while. Nothing is too good for Asher."

She flipped through a stack of cards near the cash register and handed me one. "Don't tell him I told you. I don't want to get on his bad side."

"Got it," I said. "While I'm here, could I pick up some rat poison?"

"You can't use rat poison at the farm, Ivy. Keats could eat a dead one and get sick. You'd be surprised how often that happens."

I looked down and noticed Keats had draped himself over my feet, looking subdued. Obviously he disapproved of the poison, too.

"It's for one of my sisters who wishes to remain nameless. Rodents are stigmatized even out here, it seems."

She smiled again. "Well, I can't help you anyway. There's been a rush on it lately and it's on back order."

"Okay, no problem." I looked over and saw Jilly was sitting alone. "Thanks for the coffee. We'll need it to get through our errands."

A few minutes later we were lurching down the road again. Once we were out of sight, I pulled over and called Brian Letsky, the name Myrtle had given me. When he heard my plea—specifically the "whatever it costs" part—he agreed to let us drop by immediately.

"I've got a bad feeling about this," Jilly said as we turned around and headed in the opposite direction. "You made this guy sound sketchy."

"Just because he has a stringy ponytail, yelled at Myrtle and creeps around a dead man's house in the dark?"

"Even one of those is cause for grave suspicion."

"Remember that I was not only creeping around Lloyd's house but picking through his belongings. I'm one stringy ponytail away from being sketchy myself."

"You were doing it for a good cause."

"Maybe he was, too. Let's keep an open mind." I glanced over at her. "I'm counting on you to use your wiles today."

"What about *your* wiles? I don't want to be pimped out anymore. I lost my confidence after what happened with Skint."

Skint was the horrible man we'd rescued Keats from two months ago. Hearing the name, Keats popped his head up from the backseat and whined. "Don't worry, buddy," I said. "He's out of our lives for good. Jilly's having flashbacks like I do sometimes."

She shuddered. "I'll do my best today. It's important to know if my charms still work."

"Oh, they still work. My brother is at the farm constantly and it isn't just to see Alvina."

"He does like my cooking, but he's not overly discriminating. It's all good to him."

A little smile played on her face that told me my brother stood a chance with her. I wasn't sure how I felt about combining friends and family but I figured the more closely woven my safety net, the softer my landing.

"Just flirt a little with Brian. With that ponytail, it probably doesn't happen often. I'll owe you."

"You already owe me." She pulled out a compact and examined her reflection. Jilly always complained about her supposedly crooked nose, but she was gorgeous by any standard and had a long string of romances behind her to prove it. "But let's add more to your tally."

Brian didn't look quite as unsavory as I remembered when he opened the door, but his expression darkened when he saw Keats. "I hate dogs," he said. "They're a collector's worst nightmare."

"My dog's training is impeccable, but of course I'd pay for anything he damaged inadvertently."

He shook his head. "That shows how little you know. Collecting isn't about money, it's about passion. The only reason I agreed to see you today is that I have two Wonder Woman figures right now. Selling one would let me add something new."

He didn't invite us in, so Jilly tossed him an easy smile. For a moment, it looked like it wouldn't land, but then a slight flush started around his collar. Brian had a hard shell, but he wasn't immune to an attractive woman. Stepping back, he let us pass and gestured to the living room. "Stay here," he said. "I don't let anyone into the gallery."

It only took a few minutes before he returned with Wonder Woman in what appeared to be the original packaging.

"Wow, she's perfect," I said, reaching for the box.

He slapped my hand away. "Don't touch. She's in pristine condition and she'll stay that way till she's out of my care."

"My brother is going to be super thrilled." I craned over to peek into the box. "I'd already talked to Lloyd Boyce about hooking me up, but you know how that went."

Brian took a step backwards, clutching Wonder Woman to his chest as if he didn't want her to see any of this. "Lloyd didn't have Wonder Woman. He wanted this one but he couldn't afford her. I even offered to trade for Iron Man. He had three of those, but do you think he'd part with any of them? No. He was a jerk and a hoarder. I don't know how he almost caught up with my collection because he was always broke."

"I guess he found a way when something like Wonder Woman came along," I said.

"Well, his impulse control was going to get him into trouble," Brian said. "I heard he was racking up a charge with the Scorpion. I warned him that wouldn't end well." His eyes never left Jilly's smile, as if spellbound. "Maybe it didn't."

"Maybe," I said. "I wonder who's going to get Lloyd's

collection. Nadine will need to sell it off at some point, after the smoke clears. The sooner the murder is resolved, the better."

He dragged his eyes away from Jilly and stared at me, dazed. "Maybe I'll get my hands on one of the Iron Man figures. I have pretty much everything else Lloyd had, though." After a second he added, "Someone should go down to Rattlesnake Tattoos and talk to the Scorpion. I bet he knows something."

"Have you mentioned that to the police?" I asked. "I'm sure any tip would be welcome."

He took another step back. "I'm not getting anywhere near the Scorpion. He's probably a suspect. I probably would be too if I hadn't been out of town. Lloyd and I had some disagreements."

"Chief Harper would want to know about that," I said.

Again he shook his head. "I want to stay out of it. You could just tell Asher about the Scorpion, right?"

"He got pulled off the case, unfortunately. That's why I'm splashing out on Wonder Woman for his birthday to cheer him up. So I guess all that's left is agreeing on terms."

Jilly kept the smile dialled up and I like to think that eased Brian's disappointment when I yelped in horror at the price. There was no way I could afford that kind of money for a doll my brother didn't even want. Besides, I'd learned all I needed. It seemed unlikely that Brian had killed Lloyd for his collection. At worst, he was trying to score an easy Iron Man.

"Think about it," he said, as we left. "Asher would be a lucky man to get this."

"No question. But I don't know if his ratings are that high this year."

"Talk to the police, okay?" Jilly called back with another fetching smile. "Bring Iron Man home where he belongs."

"I will," he called after her. "Come back and see him."

Jilly had to shoo Keats out of the passenger seat because he beat her inside and then pretended not to see her. "Dude, I earned that seat," she said. "You're a good sidekick, but some things are better left to a woman."

CHAPTER SIXTEEN

"Butterflies?" the young man said, raising a heavy load of metal studs on his eyebrow. "You know where you are, right?"

"Of course we know where we are," Jilly said. "The best tattoo parlour in Clover Grove."

"The *only* tattoo shop in town. We don't call it a parlour, though, and we don't do butterflies."

"Oh, come on," I said. "Women like tattoos, too." I scrolled through the samples on their laptop. "You can't tell me everyone wants scorpions and reptiles."

"That's our speciality. You'd have more luck over in Dorset Hills. Someone runs a shop catering to girls."

I glanced at Jilly and grinned. "That one's a parlour, I guess."

Resting her elbows on the counter, she turned up the smile wattage. "I'm quite sure Mr. Scorpion could do a pair of butterflies for two best friends like us. Given the complexity of most of his work, this would be a walk in the park."

"That's where he is, actually. Taking a walk in the park with his dog, like he is every day at this time." He gestured to the door. "If you want to convince him to do butterflies, go give it a try."

"Challenge accepted," I said. "Keats could use a run anyway. Which park?"

The young man gave me directions to one of the four dog parks in town. It surprised me that Clover Grove had so many, given its small population and close proximity to beautiful trails. It was another spillover effect from being neighbors with Dorset Hills.

As we walked back to the truck, I shook my head. "I wouldn't have pegged the Scorpion for a dog park kind of guy. He has a snake tat coiled around his bald head. It's terrifying. Especially when you've recently been groping around in a snake tank."

"Guess you can't judge by appearances," Jilly said, smoothing her already perfect hair. It was obvious from her appearance that no ink would ever mar her pale skin. I liked to think my chances with the Scorpion were slightly better. Since arriving in Clover Grove, my dress code had gone out the window and it was a good day when I managed anything nicer than the jeans and T-shirt I wore today.

"Maybe not, but you *can* judge by how someone treats their dog," I said as we drove the few blocks to the park. "And if the Scorpion is taking his dog to the park every day, he's not a murderer."

She laughed. "I bet many murderers are skilled with deception."

"You can't fake this," I said. "You'll see. And Keats will prove it."

"Yeah? How?"

"He can smell a fake from a mile away. Just watch his posture—his ears and tail go down when someone isn't a legit dog lover or a decent person. He can't even hide his contempt for them."

She turned to stare at me. "You know I love you, but you've gotten a bit weird since Keats came along."

"I was weird before Keats came along. I just hid it better."

"Okay, well... Maybe keep this kind of talk to yourself once you have guests at the inn."

I turned to catch her eye. "There's nothing wrong with a quirky innkeeper. Not in Clover Grove. In fact, I think that might even be a plus."

"Yeah?"

"Sure. People love to share stories about eccentrics." I pulled up at the curb and parked. "I won't lose business from talking to my animals. But murder is another matter. I don't want my guests worrying about being killed in their sleep."

"Even your former colleagues?" she asked, getting out of the truck. "A little scare might do them good."

Jilly was so incensed over Flordale burning me that she had severed ties with them at a significant financial loss. I'd tried to convince her not to burn bridges on my account, but there was no telling Jilly how to be a friend.

Coming around the truck, I couldn't help grinning. "Scaring the crap out of the Flordale people would make me pretty happy, actually. But I need good reviews."

"You don't need their help. This place is going to take off like a rocket. You can trust my instincts. And my cooking."

"I do, my friend. Just like I trust Keats' instincts."

"Please don't compare me to your dog."

I signalled Keats to run ahead and he gave me what looked like a glare. He was not the kind of dog to enjoy dog parks, where he was forced to socialize with canine riffraff. Dog park dogs tended to be rude, whereas dogs on the trails showed respect.

"Just suck it up, Keats," I said. "We all have to make sacrifices."

But then I snapped my fingers for Keats to return to my side. The tattooed man I'd seen at Myrtle's Store was standing with a group of people. They were surrounded by dogs, and I guessed immediately that the rottweiler belonged to the tattoo artist. Most of the dogs were roughhousing but none were as rambunctious as those I'd seen elsewhere. That spoke volumes about the clutch of people. Dogs behaved as owners allowed.

"Let's mingle," I said, as a few dogs frolicked up to meet Keats. He stood perfectly still, allowing the other dogs to sniff him, but indicating in dog language that they were beneath his notice. The rottweiler ambled over and offered a polite greeting.

An older woman joined us with a friendly smile. "Gorgeous border collie," she said. "He thinks he's above the rest of them, doesn't he?"

I laughed. "Is it that obvious?"

"A real sheepdog usually can't be bothered with other dogs," she said, reaching down to pat the rottie's hind end. "That said, my Roswell likes to keep his own counsel, too."

"The rottie's yours?" I said. "I was sure he belonged to—"

"Graham? The man with tattoos?" she said. "You can't judge a man by appearances."

"No, of course not," I said, avoiding Jilly's I-told-you-so gaze. "We've heard a lot about his talent and wanted to chat to him about getting some ink done."

"He doesn't like mixing business with dogs, I can tell you that," the woman said. "You're better to hit him up down at Rattlesnake Tattoos."

"We just came from there and his assistant was discouraging. I thought if we could bond over dogs, he might agree to work with us."

"Worth a try, I guess." She pointed at a small white crossbreed of indeterminate origin. "That's his sweet Charlotte."

"What breed is she?" I asked.

A middle-aged man with a prodigious mustache joined us with a genial smile. He tried to pat Keats, who literally shrank under his hand in disdain.

"A rescue from the Caribbean," she said. "A lovely dog that he treats like a queen. He brings her here every single day, rain or shine. We have a regular dog party from four to five thirty."

"Every day? I tried to find him here on Monday and didn't see him. Maybe I came too late."

"Monday?" Her eyes studied the horizon before she nodded. "Yes, we had full attendance on Monday. We're planning a little fundraiser for rescues and Graham offered to do the marketing materials."

"I remember," the moustachioed man said. "He's a graphic designer, too."

"A man of many talents," I said, following as she led us to the group. My eyes were on Keats rather than the Scorpion. The dog quickly circled the small group, taking their measure. His ears stayed up and his tail at a perfectly respectable half-mast. No one, including the Scorpion, gave him cause for concern.

"I'll introduce you," the woman said.

The Scorpion turned and eyed me suspiciously. Maybe it was impossible to look any other way when a yellow snake slithered around your head and a blue scorpion sat on your eyebrow. If I could stop judging by appearances, it was possible I'd discover he was a sweetheart, like his friends said.

"I know you," he said, his voice as chilly as the cold-blooded snake circling his ear. "You're the one who killed Lloyd Boyce."

"I most certainly did not!" The words shot out of my mouth. "Do you think I'd be hanging around at the park with my dog if that were true?"

He stared at me with fierce amber eyes that were also like a snake's, only without the vertical slits. They fell to Keats and he let out a sigh. "I guess not. Looks like a good dog. No one who loves dogs can be a murderer."

"Funny, I've heard others say the same thing," Jilly said. "Seems like a truth universally understood."

He gave her a stare that forced her to back up a step. "It is. If you owned one, you'd know."

"Agreed," I said. "Someone can be an ass, but if he's an ass who loves dogs, he's redeemable."

The Scorpion nodded grudgingly. "Pretty much."

"But Lloyd Boyce didn't love dogs."

"You don't know that," the Scorpion said. "He wasn't a bad guy, really. He just got bitten a lot on the job."

"Maybe he got bitten a lot because he didn't like dogs and they knew it. People have told me he snared dogs with a noose and hauled them away from their families. He carried pepper spray and an electric prod. I saw that with my own eyes."

The Scorpion shifted uncomfortably and his little white dog ran over. Scooping her up, he kissed her head hard. "I don't want to hear about that."

"I'm just saying that Lloyd probably wasn't as good a guy as you think."

"I know he wasn't a saint," the Scorpion said. "He owed me five grand I'll probably never see again."

"You're not the only one he wronged, obviously. Someone actually wanted him dead."

Hugging Charlotte close, he shook his head. "Sometimes I hate people. You never know what they're hiding. With a dog you know where you stand."

I nodded. "I know exactly what you mean." Pulling out my phone, I said, "That's me. We've gotta run, unfortunately. I'll catch up with you folks another day."

The older woman called out, "I thought you wanted to talk about tattoos."

Jilly turned and called back, "Cold feet."

"I don't blame you at all," the woman called after us. "Ink is so permanent."

"Exactly," I chimed in. "I'm a firm believer in leaving room to change your mind."

"I only work on people who can commit anyway," the Scorpion shouted.

Waiting till we were out of earshot, Jilly said, "That was it? You barely questioned him."

"No need. Keats questioned him for me. If the Scorpion had been on my property, Keats would have known it. His nose never forgets."

"Seriously? You trust the dog that much?"

"That much and more." I opened the passenger door and Keats jumped through to the back seat. "I trust him with my life."

CHAPTER SEVENTEEN

Jilly wasn't one of those people who wore yoga gear 24-7 for comfort and style. She'd earned the right to wear those cute outfits with years of practice back in Boston. There'd always been a rolled-up mat sticking out of her bag, even when she was wearing her best suit and heading off to meet with a corporate CEO. In fact, she credited yoga with making her more effective in her job. No bigwig could faze her when she'd put in her mat time.

My refusal to drink the yoga Kool-Aid was one of her biggest disappointments. She just wanted to share the joy and tranquility with me, her best friend. Yet I continued to maintain that anxiety and neurosis had driven me to the top of my HR game. We all find our own way up the mountain, I'd said.

That explained her Cheshire Cat smile as she rode shotgun on the way to Serenity Yoga Studio. For once, she had the seat entirely to herself. There was no white paw gently and slyly trying to usurp her. Keats and his boundless energy were even further beyond the help of yoga than I was, so for once he'd stayed home.

"Don't get your hopes up," I said as we slowed in front of the perfect parking spot. "This isn't going to stick. I'm here to interview Hayden, that's all."

She stayed quiet as I made my first attempt to parallel park. The truck stalled with its nose out, blocking traffic, and I cursed quietly. Sometimes it seemed like the vehicle was possessed.

"I was just thinking that yoga and a solid meditation practice might help with your driving."

"My driving!" I pulled out and manoeuvred into position for another attempt. "How do you figure?"

"Well, I notice that the more stressed you are, the more you stall the truck. If I keep you distracted, you do pretty well."

The next attempt was such a spectacular fail that I gave up and drove down the block to a double space. "Charlie told me that Hannah Pemberton struggled with driving stick as well. I think it's the truck."

Jilly laughed. "Okay. You can delude yourself or you can just manage your stress better."

I managed to pull the truck close enough to the curb that it wasn't totally humiliating. Still, an old man smirked as he passed. A trickle of sweat ran down my cheek. Of all of my struggles in recent weeks, my driving challenges may have taken the biggest toll. Well, other than feeding the snakes, perhaps.

"I'm shocked you'd use my biggest weakness against me, Jilly. I thought we were besties."

She laughed again and patted my arm. "Driving stick

isn't your biggest weakness. But yoga would help with your pride, too."

"Pride? I left that in Boston. Here, I'm just a humble country girl."

"From where I sit—in Keats' seat—pride is what's keeping you from joining forces with Chief Harper. Maybe this mystery would be solved by now if you two pooled your knowledge."

I pulled my bag out of the back seat with so much force that the rolled-up mat poked me in the eye and it started streaming. "Chief Harper has warned me in no uncertain terms about getting involved. He's hardly going to welcome me as his backup."

"He just wants you to stay safe. There's still a murderer at large, in case you've forgotten."

"Are you trying to jack up the tension so that I get more out of our private yoga session?"

"More tension would make your still-recovering brain explode," she said, opening the door. "I'm just saying that it wouldn't be a bad idea to get over your broken heart and team up with Chief Hottie."

We walked back down the block to Serenity Yoga Studio. "My heart isn't broken anymore. It's just off-line for now. I've got way too much to worry about without that."

She tipped her face to the sky and her hair rippled down her back. Her cheery disposition reminded me of sunflowers. Clover Grove was bringing out the best in her, and she'd apparently given up her flat iron for good. But the clean country air hadn't dulled her mind one bit.

"Your heart's been off-line since we met," she said.

"And now I know why. Chief Hottie stole it early and never let it go."

Pressing my lips together, I studied the cute and kitschy shops that had replaced the familiar stores of my youth. The hardware store had become The Tipsy Grape, a wine bar. Mark's Grocery was now Fresh on the Fork, and the seamstress who'd made prom gowns for nearly every girl in high school had retired to make way for Cheeky Cheats Chocolatier.

"He did steal it early," I said at last. "He was different in high school. Lighter. Fun."

"What happened?" Jilly's voice was soft, as if stepping through a field of land mines.

"Different colleges," I said. "We thought we could make it work long distance but we ended up a cliché with the turkey dump." I debated about adding the truth and decided to take the plunge. "He thought I cheated on him. One of our high school classmates told him so, and he believed him over me."

Jilly's gasp eased the surprisingly sharp pain that welled up in my chest. "How could he?" she asked. "You're honest and loyal and I assume that was the case then, too."

"The other guy obviously told a good story. And I refused to grovel to convince Kellan if he didn't want to believe me." I shoved my shoulders back and raised my chin. "It was for the best, Jilly. I wouldn't have had the career I did if we'd come home together after college like we planned. I wouldn't have the farm now, and I wouldn't have Keats." I gave her a smile. "You know I've never been particularly woo-woo, but it feels like everything unfolded as it should have."

She opened the door to Serenity Yoga Studio. "Well, let's unfold those yoga mats and see if we can clear the path to your happily ever after."

"So, no pressure," I said, leading her up the stairs to the airy, open space.

"Pressure is the enemy of peace," someone said as we entered the room. I turned to see a handsome man who was probably around 40 but looked far younger. He walked toward us with the elegance of a ballet dancer and his clear blue eyes seemed to see into my yoga-hating soul. He held out his hand and said, "I'm Hayden Rockwood."

I shook his hand, surprised at his firm grip. "I'm Ivy, the doubter, and this is Jilly, the believer. She knows the magic of yoga well."

His smile showed perfect teeth and for a second it felt like my heart might not be dead after all. I shook my head to dispel the notion and glanced at Jilly. She had the same dopey look I felt on my features.

"I welcome the chance to convert you," he said, smiling even harder. "A private session will give us a chance to figure out what class is best for you."

The next hour was complete torture. With all the hard labor I'd been doing on the farm I figured I was in peak form but it didn't translate into a sunrise salutation, let alone the revolved triangle pose. Jilly alternated between giggling at me and turning serious again when Hayden's intense gaze reminded her that the practice of yoga was no joke.

"Oh man," I said, finally collapsing on my back. "I feel something, but it's more like nausea than peace and serenity."

"You did great," Hayden said, without a trace of mockery. "Obviously Jilly has technical proficiency, but it seemed like you were really channeling spirit and that will take you far."

"Channeling spirit. That's what I want." I sat up and smiled. "I heard the hot yoga class will clear out all the blocks and bring on the spirit."

"Definitely. But it's more advanced than you might enjoy right now," he said. "Given the nausea."

"You're probably right," Jilly said. "But she's got to see it to believe it. You livestream classes, right? I saw one on your social media page. How about showing Ivy the misery of hot yoga?"

"Sure." Rising gracefully, he led us out of the room to the front desk. There, he cued up the laptop and showed us a video capture. I bent over the screen to study it more closely and saw Nadine Boyce in the front row.

Jilly beckoned to Hayden. "Would you mind giving me support for my headstand? I felt some pain in my neck earlier and I don't want to end up paralyzed."

"No one breaks her neck at Serenity Yoga Studio," he said, leading Jilly back to her mat.

I worked quickly, finding the footage from the day of Lloyd's murder. There were eight fit bodies sweating it out in the five p.m. hot yoga class... and none of them belonged to Nadine.

When they returned I was watching footage from the

day before. Hayden leaned over me and said, "What do you think?"

I pressed pause at precisely the point where Hayden had bent over Nadine with his hands resting on her hips. Both of them had silly smiles on their faces.

"I think it looks like fun," I said. "Nadine Boyce could be the poster girl for hot yoga."

Jilly leaned in for a look. "Hot indeed."

Hayden's handsome face had flushed. "It's just a normal correction. Nadine and I have worked together a long time so we're casual."

"Casual," I repeated. "Nothing wrong with casual between two single yogis."

"It's not like that," he said, sounding alarmed. "We have a policy here about dating students."

"Shame that," Jilly said, sticking her rolled-up mat back in her bag. "It's probably hard to find spiritually minded souls in this town."

"Don't worry," I said, leading her out. "Maybe there's a hill country dating site where we can find you a self-actualized farmer. I'm sure there are one or two."

"All it takes is one," she said, smiling.

"Thanks, Hayden," I called back up the stairs. "That was totally enlightening."

"AFTER ALL THAT relaxation I need a walk with my bestie," I said, parking the truck outside the barn.

"You got it," Jilly said. "Although I'd rather get back

to the kitchen. Sleuthing with you is costing me valuable recipe testing time."

I laughed. "Run to your spatulas. I meant my other bestie, anyway."

"Ah, the truth comes out. I've become a distant second to Keats. I'm only useful when dogs aren't permitted."

"Untrue," I said, grinning. "But I will say that Keats never asks me probing questions about my past. He leaves memories alone that are better buried."

"And he probably won't remind you to call Chief Hottie to tell him Nadine's alibi is full of manure."

"Keats trusts my judgement implicitly."

The dog was howling in the house as if his heart had broken. He wasn't used to being left behind.

"Sounds like it," Jilly said, heading up the path. "I'll let him out and you can make it up to him in the fields. But listen to your second-best friend, Ivy: call the cops."

I started down the trail that led to the meadow. "Got it, second-bestie. Stop nagging and you might make it back to top dog."

"And be careful," she yelled after me. "It'll be dark in an hour or so."

"I've got my pepper spray," I said, waving my fanny pack before putting it on. Before farm life, I'd judged fanny packs far too harshly. They came in very handy.

Keats caught up to me fast and all was forgiven as he raced through the long grass. He sank to his belly, leapt in the air and flushed out a rabbit. Just for fun, he chased it and tried to herd it with evident joy and no success. His antics made me smile. This was exactly what I'd dreamed about when I rescued him two months ago.

Just as suddenly, however, he circled my legs and drove me backwards so abruptly I almost stumbled. "What is it, boy?"

He ran back and forth in front of me to keep me from advancing. I picked up a long stick and swept the grass back to expose a deep hole about two feet wide. Switching on my phone light I stared down into the deep cavity and saw nothing but roots. The soil piled at the side was still dark and moist, as if the hole were freshly dug.

"That's odd," I said. "We could have broken a leg."

I used the stick and Keats' nose to explore the rest of the area. It wasn't far from where Lloyd had died, and the field had been combed thoroughly by the police. This hole had obviously appeared after they'd ended their investigation.

Keats moved quite a ways off and after a few minutes gave a sharp little yip I'd come to know as "Discovery!"

Kneeling bedside him, I parted the grass and found what looked like a smooth, round stone. Holding it up to the setting sun, however, the rays passed right through. The milky white glass was etched with what appeared to be mountains. I guessed that the stone had been set in a ring or a pendant at one time. Probably not long ago, given its pristine condition.

"I think I've seen this somewhere," I told Keats, pocketing it. "My head is too full of facts now, buddy. I don't make connections like I used to." He gave a little whine and nudged my hand. "Don't worry, my neurons are rewiring and I'll be fully functional before you know it."

We walked back to the house and I showed the stone to Jilly, who was up to her elbows in flour as she assembled pastry for yet another quiche.

"I've seen that before," she said, dropping the rolling pin onto the counter with a clatter. "Maybe Nadine wasn't the one after all."

I picked up a ball of pastry that had splatted on the floor. "And the glop thickens."

CHAPTER EIGHTEEN

Margie Hodgson tried to close her front door in my face but I managed to get my foot in the crack first. Steel-toed work boots had proven to be a very wise investment.

"Margie, hold up," I said. "I just want to chat."

"We're busy, Ivy. I'm sorry."

"But I brought a pie," I said. "Well, a quiche actually. My friend Jilly's a whiz in the kitchen. You met her."

Margie's oversized eyeglasses appeared in the crack. "She's a nice girl."

"I'm a nice girl, too. Whatever I've done to offend you, I'm sorry, Margie."

"It's not that," she said. "I just don't want to see anybody today."

There was a shuffle of footsteps behind her. "Margie, what's going on?"

Another set of fingers appeared around the door and pulled it open to reveal both Hodgsons in matching Clover Grove souvenir sweatshirts.

"Let the girl in, for pity's sake," Fred Hodgson said. "She could drop that quiche, and despite what people say, real men do eat them."

I laughed and stepped back as the door opened. "Your lunch has arrived, Mr. Hodgson."

"Come on in and have a coffee, young lady," he said. "We were just doing the crossword. What's an eight-letter word for sapphire?"

"Gemstone?" I said, following them into the kitchen. Keats was close on my heels and sat beside me when I stopped.

Fred took a seat at the old oak table and examined the newspaper. "Nailed it!"

Margie stayed silent as she poured coffee into a mug and when I sat down, she slid it in front of me. The place had the shabby but comfortable look of a house that had been lived in and loved well. Not the home of murderers, surely.

"How come you're here and not down at Myrtle's?" I asked. "She said you two are practically fixtures."

He sighed. "Margie's gone off the place. Said she got a bad date square."

"Up all night sick," she said, fussing around the sink and clattering cutlery. Despite how flustered she was, she filled a bowl with water and put it down for Keats. He fanned his tail politely and took a few licks.

"What a shame," I said. "I love Mandy's baking. She'll be doing all my desserts at the inn when it opens."

"She's lovely. I don't blame her," Margie said. "We'll go back at some point."

"I hope so," Fred said, peering at the newspaper. "The words came easier there."

"Gimme another one," I said, sipping my coffee.

"Six-letter word for slaying?" He glanced up quickly. "Let's pass on that one."

"Murder," I offered. "Which I suppose is what's keeping you two at home these days."

"What do you mean?" Margie's voice rose over the running water.

"Well, you had strong feelings about Lloyd. You told me so yourself."

"Are you accusing us of—of murdering him?"

I shook my head. "I can't imagine that at all."

"We already told the police chief everything we know. Which is nothing," Fred said, setting down his pencil. "But Margie *has* made harsh comments about Lloyd in the past, and people talk."

"I'm not the only one who hated him for killing their dog. There's an army of us."

"Margie." Her husband's voice was soft, but insistent. "That kind of talk is what has us trapped in our kitchen. People our age need community. And quiche."

"I wouldn't have harmed a hair on Lloyd Boyce's head," Margie said. "But I won't pretend I'm not glad someone got him. He deserved it."

"*Margie!*" This time her husband rose and put a hand on her arm. "Stop."

I gestured to the seat opposite me and said, "Margie, sit down for a sec. Would you believe I'm here about something else entirely? I just want your advice on a birthday gift for my friend, Jilly." She still hung back, so I added, "What's an eight-letter word for sapphire?"

"Gemstone," she said, managing a faint smile as she perched on the edge of the old oak chair. "You want to get Jilly a sapphire?"

I laughed. "She's special but not *that* special. I understand that she liked a pendant you were wearing when you met, and I wondered if I could see it?"

Margie nodded and rose. "I know the one."

I supplied Fred with a couple of words while Margie was out of the room. She moved slowly and stiffly, and it was hard to believe she could strangle anything bigger than a mouse. When she returned, a long chain dangled from her right hand, which looked gnarled from arthritis.

"Oh, how pretty," I said, taking the pendant. The stone was similar to the one I'd found, but this was a pale pink. "It's glass, right? What's etched on it?"

"Hills," Margie said. "There's a jeweller in town who designs these to symbolize our beautiful landscape. Fred gave me this for our 50th anniversary."

"Well, there couldn't be a more perfect gift to celebrate Jilly's visit to Clover Grove," I said. "If you don't mind, that is. Imitation is the sincerest form of flattery, right?"

I took a picture of the pendant, brainstormed a few more words with them and then set off for town.

TERI MASON of Hill Country Designs greeted me with a smile when the bell rang to herald my entrance. She got up from a stool behind the counter and came around. Her spiky hair had pink and blue streaks, a bold statement for Clover Grove. I bet she had to drive 60 miles to find a stylist to pull that off. I'd already decided to grow my hair out to become lower maintenance. Priorities.

"What a beautiful dog," she said, offering the back of her hand to Keats. "That blue eye could give you chills."

Keats gave her hand a sniff and his tail rose, the white tuft offering an approving twitch.

"It does sometimes," I admitted. "I feel like he sees more than other dogs."

She squatted and let Keats come closer. "He's a mystic fox in sheepdog form. I'm getting inspired."

I laughed, looking around the shop. There were fanciful watercolor portraits of many dogs on the wall. "It would be torture for Keats to sit still for so long."

"I can do it from a photo," she said, rising. "May I?"

"I doubt many dog-owners could resist an offer to have their dogs immortalized like that. Your work is amazing."

"Thank you. I wish the paintings sold as well as some of my other work, but I paint them for love."

"I'll buy a portrait of Keats for my new inn," I said. "In fact, if you want to display some of your pieces there, I'd be honored."

Teri made a move as if to hug me and thought better of it. "The honor would be all mine. You must be Ivy Galloway from Runaway Farm. I heard you were opening the doors soon."

I nodded and pulled a card out of my pocket. "My first guests arrive in about two weeks. Why don't you come and check the place out? My sister Daisy and my friend Jilly have been giving it the final polish. Not that Hannah Pemberton left much for us to do."

"I'd love to meet the menagerie again. I went to all of Hannah's events and fell in love with the alpaca."

"Alvina has a cult following. Happily, she's adjusted well to the change. She's even fallen for my brother, Asher."

"Well, Asher has a bit of a cult following, too," Teri said, grinning. "Half of the old ladies in town call in fake emergencies in the hopes that Asher will be sent out. They almost mobilized to picket the station when he got reassigned to highway patrol."

"Seriously? Asher?" A laugh spilled out of me and Keats looked up, startled. Then his tongue lolled out one side in a happy smile. I realized then how much my stress had been wearing on him, too. We hardly smiled anymore.

"We never see our siblings as others do, right?" Teri said. "Asher's a lovely man, inside and out." She beckoned me to the counter. "Now what can I do for you today?"

"I'm looking for a birthday gift for Jilly." I pulled out the little glass stone. "I found this and someone recognized it as your work. I was thinking of a pendant."

Teri took the stone and gave a little gasp.

"Where exactly did you find it?" she asked. "I only made two of these."

I thought about evading the question, but Teri seemed like a good person. Keats thought so, which was enough for me to take a chance.

"In a field at the farm, actually. Keats nosed it out, Jilly took a shine to it and Margie Hodgson has something similar." I shrugged. "So here I am."

Teri's hand trembled as she set it on a little velvet cushion that sat on top of the display case. She looked up at me with intense dark eyes. "Like I said, I only made two of these pendants in white. Both for Lloyd Boyce. I saw Nadine wearing hers plenty of times, but I don't know what happened to the other one."

A shiver ran down my back and Keats' hackles rose at the same time. I knew exactly whose neck the other pretty pendant had graced. Giving two women the same piece was the move of a tacky man. At least he hadn't had one made for Daisy, too.

"I know about Lloyd's passing, of course," Teri said. "How do you think my little stone ended up in your field?"

"No idea," I said, picking up the stone and pocketing it. "But it's something I'll need to share with the police, Teri. I guess you can expect a call at some point."

She frowned and then smiled again. "I'll ask for Asher."

I laughed again. "You're going to get the chief, I'm afraid."

"Equally handsome but devoid of charm," she said.

"Not completely," I said, heading for the door. "He just needs the love of a good dog to bring it out."

"What about the gift for Jilly?" she called after me. "Was that a ruse?"

"Sort of, yeah," I called back. "But the offer of displaying your art was 100 percent legit."

"Good. And the offer to paint Keats also stands."

"No take-backs on something that important," I said, turning with my hand on the door. "It'll have pride of place over the mantel."

"It was nice meeting you," she said.

She tilted her spiky head a little and Keats mirrored the pose. It was a sign that he not only expected but hoped we'd meet again.

"You too," I said. "Keats welcomes you to our pack."

"Ivy, watch out for—"

CHAPTER NINETEEN

The door slammed before I caught Teri's last words but I had no trouble figuring out what she was warning me about.

Kellan Harper was standing outside the door. With his arms crossed. Waiting. There was a chill in his eyes that rivalled Keats' sole baby blue. Meanwhile, Keats' ruff came up and his tail went down and I wondered if Kellan realized how much they had in common at that moment. Telling him so wasn't going to win me any favors, however, so I gave him a bland smile.

"Hey, Chief. I was just arranging for a sitting for Keats. I'm going to hang his portrait over the mantel at my inn."

"Sounds nice," he said, with as little enthusiasm as a man can have and still be conscious. "What else were you doing?"

"Making new friends. I could use some in Clover Grove. My name is still under the cloud of death, you know. Some people are actually scared of me. As if murder on your land were contagious."

Kellan sighed. "Have you thought about delaying your opening? Just long enough to let the dust settle?"

Anger rose in my belly like a tornado and he must have felt it coming because he took a step backwards. "I am not delaying my opening. My first guests are my former colleagues. The boss who treated me like crap. The last thing I want is to look like a failure in front of him."

"Ivy, you were a corporate whiz kid. Asher was always bragging about you."

I scuffed at the pavement with my work boot. "I got written off as crazy, Kellan. The reputation I spent a decade building was ruined. My family—my mother especially—tries to pretend all that didn't happen. She speaks of 'the incident' in hushed tones." I looked up at him again. "For her, the murder is probably less of a big deal than my career downfall."

The ice in his eyes thawed noticeably and he beckoned me to walk with him. "You've been through a lot this year, but the memories will fade."

"A lot of memories faded. Permanently. But the work fiasco wasn't one of them."

"A selective concussion," he said. "Interesting. But you have no control over that."

I stared around at the shops, wondering how many people were staring back from inside. Lots, probably. Fingers were already working the keys to get the news out on the grapevine: *Murder brings high school sweethearts together again. Or does it? Stay tuned!*

Finally I said, "I take it you're no closer to figuring out what happened to Lloyd."

"I ruled out a few things," he said. "Which brings me quite a bit closer."

"What things?"

"Ivy, we talked about this. You need to stand back and be patient."

I glanced up at him. "Do you remember patience ever being one of my virtues?"

"Actually, no, come to think of it. But now you're like a... runaway camel."

"Alpaca. Or llama. There are no camels at Runaway Farm."

He stopped outside the Berry Best Café. "Do you have time for a coffee? We might as well talk about what you've been doing. You've been seen stalling your truck all over town and I bet you're still nosing around." He looked down at Keats, who'd positioned himself to my right, maintaining a protective barrier between Kellan and me. "The dog would need to stay outside."

I shook my head. "I don't leave him tied up alone like that. Past trauma."

"Past trauma?" His dark eyebrows rose.

"Yep. For both of us." I looked away to discourage further questions. "But they have a patio out back and Keats can join us there."

Kellan nodded. "I'll get you a coffee and meet you there."

I chose a round metal table in the corner where we were less likely to be overheard. Normally Keats would consider himself off duty at this point, but today he stayed on his paws, even after Kellan set two coffee mugs and a huge cranberry scone on the table and took the seat opposite.

Thanking him, I took a sip. My heart did a tiny pirouette in my chest when I realized he'd remembered exactly how I liked it after all these years. A touch of cream and about 10 grains of sugar. He tossed down a packet of sugar as insurance. I thought he looked a little proud it wasn't needed.

After taking a long swig of his own coffee, he broke off a piece of the scone, chewed and swallowed. Then he asked, "So, what do you know?"

He pushed the scone toward me and I broke off a piece and tried it. "I know this isn't as good as Mandy McCain's scones. She's the best baker in Clover Grove." When he didn't respond I added, "Did you confirm whether Lloyd was seeing Mandy?"

"Depends what you consider 'seeing.' Lloyd may have had big plans but I don't think he'd made much progress."

I pulled the glass stone out of my pocket and set it on the table in front of him. "Lloyd bought two pendants with this stone—the only two like it. One of them belongs to Nadine, according to the designer. I'm pretty sure I saw the other one on Mandy."

He turned the small stone with big fingers. "Where'd you find it?"

"In my fields, not far from where... you know." I pulled out my phone and scrolled through photos for him. "And this is the big hole someone dug for no apparent reason, other than maybe breaking my leg. Or burying some evidence."

Increasing the size of the image, he pressed his lips together. "You were going to tell me about this when?"

"Soon. I was just trying to—"

He pushed the scone toward me. "Get your leg broken? Or worse?"

I pushed the scone back. "Keats wouldn't let that happen. He sniffed it out."

"He didn't stop Charlie from getting injured." Kellan shoved the scone toward me again.

"He would have if he'd had the opportunity. He was inside." I shoved the scone back once more. It was getting a lot of miles on it for an average scone.

"How many accidents does it take for you to realize you're at risk?" he asked. "And now you want to put your guests at risk, too. Does that make sense to you?"

I stared into my coffee cup. "What makes sense is solving this murder fast. So I have to do what I can, Kellan."

He sighed. "What else have you found? Be honest, Ivy. Maybe you've got something I don't."

"Well, now you have the stone, and Teri Mason can confirm what I told you. My best guess is that Nadine was wearing her necklace when she choked Lloyd and he ripped it off."

"She has an alibi, remember."

"It's full of holes." I told him about the private yoga session Jilly and I'd had with Hayden.

"I checked the building's security footage," Kellan

said. "Nadine arrived at the studio that day at four and left at eight."

"Maybe, but she wasn't in the hot yoga class like they told you. She's been putting in lots of extra time getting her poses right with Hayden, though. Did she mention that?"

He pressed his lips together in a silent "no" and avoided my eyes.

I took another bite of the travelling scone and said, "Obviously he's covering for Nadine. Go back and check the live feed for the class. And then ask about her necklace. See if it's missing in action."

"Yes, boss," he said, frowning. "Anything else?"

"She's running low on rat poison. I saw it in her shopping basket at Myrtle's before Lloyd died. I wondered if she was poisoning the mice in hopes of killing the snakes but maybe she had bigger plans."

"I doubt that. Although the baked goods in Lloyd's fridge came back clean and we couldn't find any other traces in the kitchen. Mandy's off the hook on that front."

"Check the mice. But I certainly hope he wasn't eating *them*."

"There wasn't enough poison in his system to do more than give him a bellyache," Kellan said. "The final autopsy report said the bruising on Lloyd's neck was consistent with the sheep hook. But he was mostly likely strangled with wire. It would have taken a lot of strength and dexterity, and the killer likely struck from above."

"I thought about the guy from Rattlesnake Tattoos. Lloyd owed him five grand. But Jilly and I checked him out and he's clean." I plucked out a few cranberries. "Well, not a murderer, anyway."

"And you know that how?"

"Because he loves his dog."

"That means nothing."

"Of course it means something. It means everything. No man who loves his dog that much could murder someone." I put my hand over my heart. "Those two things can't coexist."

"I'd like to refute that and I will," he said, taking another piece of scone.

"Well, you can present your findings. In the meantime, the Scorpion has a quality alibi. Several people at the dog park saw him at the time of the murder. No way he could have gotten to the farm to clobber Lloyd."

"A quality alibi?"

"Exactly. I'm not so sure about Brian Letsky's. He wanted Lloyd's Iron Man doll so he was at least somewhat motivated. But he claims he was away for the weekend."

Kellan had stopped chewing and I didn't think he had swallowed.

"Maybe you could verify his alibi," I continued. "I don't think Iron Man alone was sufficient motive to kill. There are plenty on the market. But he and Lloyd had a not-so-friendly competition going, and I saw him creeping at Lloyd's the first night I went in. When you showed up, he fled like a— Well, like I did, I guess."

"You went to Lloyd's place at night?"

"Just in and out. No biggie." I gave him a sheepish smile and it looked like he was struggling to swallow his mouthful of scone. Finally he washed it down with coffee.

"You and Jilly have been busy," he said.

"We've talked to a few people, that's all. It's hard to imagine Brian jumping on Lloyd and choking him. He's a nerd, but I guess anything is possible."

Kellan looked like he wasn't sure whether to laugh or scowl. "How did you get onto Brian?"

"After I found the dolls at Lloyd's I asked around about who collected action figures and such, and deployed Jilly to flirt the information out of him. It wasn't that hard, really. It's always disappointing when the leads don't pan out, though. You get your hopes up and... splat."

"Tell me about it." He pushed the scone aside. "Brian's alibi checked out, for your information. He was at a comic con in Boston that weekend."

I pulled the scone toward me. It wasn't amazing, but there was no sense letting baked goods go to waste.

"So it sounds like we've come full circle to Nadine again. She wanted to get their divorce settled so she could enjoy perpetual sweltering peace with Hayden. Meanwhile Lloyd was bleeding down their assets."

"It's not Nadine. You and your mutt are barking up the wrong tree."

Keats shifted his position so that he could cast his baleful blue eye on Kellan.

"She hasn't been upfront about what she was doing the night Lloyd died," I said. "Maybe she left from another door and came back. Doesn't that warrant taking another look?"

"Oh, I'll be taking another look," he said. "You've given me more to think about, I must admit. And your speed is impressive."

"Thank you." His tone didn't sound complimentary but I decided to run with it.

"But there's more to police work than speed, Ivy. You may have undercut my methodical questioning with your hit-and-run conversations. This kind of investigation takes time and care."

His disapproval hung over the table like a bad smell. "I don't have time, Kellan. This is just a job to you, whereas my whole future hangs in the balance."

He sat back in his chair as if he'd been struck. "This isn't just a job to me. It's my calling."

"I'm sorry. I didn't mean it that way. I'm just really invested in getting this sorted out, as you can imagine."

"I'm equally invested, I assure you. And that means protecting people like you from yourself."

"I don't need protection."

"Ivy." He leaned both elbows on the table and stared at me so fiercely I had to look down and brush crumbs onto the patio stones. Normally Keats would be all over them, but not today. "I can't believe what you've been doing the past few days," he said. "You're unstoppable. Reckless. You didn't used to be this way."

"You're right about that," I said, hearing the bitterness in my own voice.

"You blame this on your accident?"

"Directly and indirectly, I suppose." I let my index finger trace from one dent in the table to another. "Getting attacked changes you. It's taking months to recover.

My old life ended so I decided to start over with Keats. That was how I was going to salvage something from the whole thing. When Hannah Pemberton offered me this wonderful farm for a price I could afford—barely—it seemed like fate intervening. It turns out fate has a terrible sense of humor."

He touched my sleeve lightly and I jumped. A trail of tiny sparks seemed to travel up my arm and bring heat to my cheeks. "Leave it to me, Ivy," he said. "I will get to the bottom of this, and sooner than you think."

"Kellan, I respect you and your work, really I do. But I'm done leaving my fate in the hands of... well, fate. Whatever I can do to protect my animals, property, friends, and family, I've got to do it."

"I understand," he said. "And that's why I'm telling you now that I will lock you up if you get into one more situation."

"I'm not doing anything illegal," I said. "You have no cause."

Getting up, he gave a snort that was supposed to pass for a laugh. "I'll find cause. It's my duty to protect citizens by whatever means necessary."

"Well, I'm not going to insult you by lying to you and saying I'll stand down."

"And I'm not going to lie to you and say I won't take action."

I got up, too. "No action could deter me."

"Not even talking to your mother?" His eyebrows rose and dared me.

I frowned. "Please don't. I can't bear her exploding into a million pieces when she gets home."

"And I can't bear telling her or your brother that I haven't kept you safe," he said.

There was a long moment where something else hung in the air over us—something that felt both magical and frightening. It was almost unbearable, so I broke the silence.

"I don't remember what safe feels like anymore, Kellan. So I figure I don't have much to lose by trying."

The feeling of connection vanished and he shook his head. "Then let me *give* you something to lose, Ivy. If you continue to impede my investigation, I will have your dog impounded."

My gasp was loud enough to startle Keats. "You'd never!"

"Try me," he said. "If you get into one more dangerous exploit without informing me, that dog is mine."

Tears filled my eyes. "That's a terrible thing to say."

"Then say what I need to hear."

Leaning down, I wrapped one arm around Keats. "I will keep you posted on everything even remotely related to the case until this killer is caught."

CHAPTER TWENTY

"I don't know what I ever saw in him, Keats," I said, as we wandered through the meadow beyond the barn later that day. "Back in school he was a good guy. A really good guy. All the girls wanted him, you know. I was surprised he even noticed me."

I hurled a stick for Keats and he ran after it. His energy was only at 30 or 40 percent, however, which meant he had things on his mind, too. Thinking back, I realized he'd never been truly playful since we arrived here. It was one worry after the next for both of us. Retrieving the stick, he dropped it out of reach with a sheepish wag to let me know he appreciated my efforts but he wasn't interested in games.

"Got it, buddy," I said. "Then I'll just continue musing if you don't mind."

His tail came up and he offered his peculiar mumbled response.

"I'll take that as a yes, my poet. Feel free to chime in as you see fit." We passed the spot where Keats had found

Lloyd and a shudder ran through me. No matter how often I walked in the fields—and I hoped it would be daily in the coming years—I'd never forget the sight of those boots pointing toward a sunset sky on an evening just like this one.

"So, as I was saying, Kellan Harper has turned into a jerk. Everyone changes over 15 years, and I'm no exception, obviously. But the guy I liked back then would never have threatened any dog, let alone my dog. It's inexcusable."

Keats mumbled agreement and nudged my hand.

"He said he loved me, you know. I didn't take it too seriously. Guys blurt those things out." I looked down and Keats was giving me the blue-eyed stare. "Yes, if you must know, I said it back." I shook my head and grinned. "Don't ask me if I meant it. I probably did at the time, but you can't hold me to something I said at 18."

He turned to add his brown eye—the compassionate one—to the gaze. I sighed and then continued. "Thanks, my friend. It's hard seeing how he feels about me now. He thinks I'm a crazy wild card with no common sense at all. Me... the one who was the epitome of logic, until you came along."

Panting anxiously, he gave a low moan that seemed to end with a question mark.

"Never," I said. "Not for one second do I regret what happened when I rescued you. I'd do it again tomorrow, and the next day and every day after that. Of course, by then there wouldn't be much brain power left in me. But I'd do what I could."

His mouth relaxed into a sloppy smile and his tail

fanned, the white tip almost glowing in the gorgeous waning sun.

"It'll all be fine, Keats, I'm sure of it. We just need to keep on plodding forward." We had plodded forward—farther than I'd been before on foot. I'd covered the property a few times on an ATV with Charlie but it felt different on my own. There were coyotes and foxes around, and maybe a murderer, too. That's why I had the pepper spray and even a jackknife in my fanny pack. But it was time to turn back. It would be nearly dark when we reached the house.

The back of my neck prickled and the hairs rose on my arm. I looked down and saw Keats was on alert, too. His ruff was up and his ears forward. Long nose rising, he sniffed the air. A few more paces and his nose came down to the grass. Then he circled in front of me, drawing in snorting gusts. He'd found some kind of trail that was far more interesting than rabbit.

"Keats, wait," I said. "It's almost dusk. We can come back tomorrow and sniff around."

He hesitated and then took another few steps forward. He rarely disobeyed, and I liked to think that when he did, it was for a good reason.

"Okay, just a little further. But I'm calling Jilly so that if something happens, she's aware."

There was a clatter of pots against stainless steel when Jilly picked up.

"Hey. Where are you?" She put the phone on speaker and continued washing up from yet another culinary experiment. "Dinner's ready. You are going to love my chicken with tomato and basil. It's a winner, and luckily, just as good reheated when you show up."

My stomach grumbled at the thought of it. "We'll be back soon. Keats is tracking a scent and I got a little spooked."

"Out in the fields where Lloyd died? Is that a surprise? Come home and start again in the morning."

"It's going to rain and he'll lose the trail. He really wants to get the job done now."

Jilly sighed. "Which is exactly what you promised Kellan not to do, correct?"

"Can we not talk about him right now? I'm still traumatized over what he said."

"But not traumatized enough to stay safe in the house."

"When I'm upset I walk. If we happen to stumble on a clue, I'm sure that jerk will give us a pass when I share it with him. I doubt he meant it, anyway. He's just trying to scare me."

"Poor man doesn't know how hard it is to scare you these days."

I laughed. "True that. I was a shrinking violet in high school. If Asher hadn't brought Kellan home to shoot hoops all the time we wouldn't have met. Daisy had me under such close watch I'd never had so much as a date. And really, we didn't have a proper date till prom. We just started hanging out when Asher got distracted. Which was often, as you can imagine."

"Finally, I get the story." The banging of pots and pans ended as she gave me her full attention. She was as distractible as Asher in her own way, but a whiff of romance gave her laser focus. "A slow, organic growth that bloomed by prom."

"Pretty much, yeah. Back then, he wanted to be a lawyer. Neither one of us came from money so we had to grab the scholarships on offer. He went to UCLA for football, and I went north, as you know." I pulled a small bright flashlight out of my fanny pack and shone it after Keats. "Long distance never works."

"You came home at Thanksgiving and he'd heard you were seeing someone else."

"Yeah. Unbeknownst to me, Asher asked another guy to keep an eye on me at college. We were just pals, but the guy caught feelings and lied to Kellan that I shared them."

"And he wouldn't listen to reason?"

I shook my head then realized she couldn't hear me. "No. Maybe it confirmed his worst fears. I figured it would work itself out during the summer when we came home. But he didn't come home. He got a job there and stayed." I shone the light around and caught sight of Keats far ahead. "That was that."

"Till now," Jilly said. "You've got a second chance. He doesn't seem happy single."

"I'm not giving him a second chance after threatening my dog."

"He's trying to keep both of you safe, that's all. Can you blame him? The sun is almost down and you're walking around in a field where you found a big hole this week."

"It's okay, we're there," I said.

"Where's 'there'?"

"Not sure yet, but Keats is pointing. Do you know he has the best traits of all breeds? Tracking, retrieving, pointing, herding. The only thing he hates is water."

"Can we rave over Keats later? Figure out what he's found and come home, Ivy. You might not be scared, but I am."

Keats held one white forepaw up and close to his chest. His long nose was aimed at what first appeared to be a small pile of rocks almost surrounded by scrub brush. As I got closer, I saw the rocks circled corroding bricks in the shape of a circle. Old, mossy boards lay overtop.

"Oh wow," I said. "It looks like an old well."

"Stay back," Jilly said. "'Old' means dangerous and 'well' means deep hole. And water."

"The boards covering it are rotting, but it looks like one of them has been moved recently. Keats certainly thinks so."

The dog kept sniffing around the base, moving out in concentric circles. Finally he stopped and the paw rose again. I stooped and aimed the flashlight.

"What is it?" Jilly's voice was high and tight.

"A footprint. A bit bigger than mine, but not much. A woman found this old well recently."

"What would someone want with your old well?"

"Seems like a perfect place for a murder weapon to me," I answered. "I'll get Charlie to drag it tomorrow."

"And you'll tell Kellan, right?"

"I most certainly will, Jilly. You can count on that."

There was such conviction in my voice that she didn't bother to press me for a timeframe.

"Come home right now," she said. "Or I'll call him myself."

"I'm on my way. I'll stick to the trail and talk to you all the way back. Meanwhile, you can heat up some of that basil chicken. Although I've got to admit my enthusiasm for chicken has faded a bit since I got my own flock of hens."

"This new simple life is rife with conflict, isn't it?" she said. "It's a good thing we know how to compartmentalize."

"That's one skill we brought over from corporate life," I said. "Glad I got something out of it."

CHAPTER TWENTY-ONE

Jilly had arrived in Clover Grove with a small suitcase. Despite how busy we'd been, she'd managed to check out the shops around town and discover a few finds, including a black dress that said both "classy night out" and "funeral." I'd given away most of my corporate wardrobe before leaving Boston, but luckily I kept one charcoal lightweight wool jacket and pants. The second I put them on I felt sucked into my past life. On the bright side, I wasn't likely to stand out in the crowd at Lloyd Boyce's funeral, or rather, "celebration of life." I'd been of two minds whether to go or not, but it seemed like people might talk more if I avoided it. As much as I hated that gossip had become a factor in my life now, I'd have to pay attention to it until my inn was established.

"You okay?" Jilly asked as we walked up the stairs and into the vestibule of the only funeral home in town. Most people still opted for churches in Clover Grove, and there were plenty of those. I assumed Nadine

wanted to keep the event low profile, given the circumstances.

"Yeah, sure. I just miss Keats." Turning, I added, "No
offence. You know how glad I am you're here. It's just
that crowds still make me anxious."

"It's the suit making you anxious," she said. "You
should have dropped it down the well after you dragged
it."

I laughed. "Thank god Charlie was well enough to
ride out and take care of it. I didn't want Gwen to know."

"I thought you trusted Gwen. She's been great with
the animals."

"That she has. But she is a woman with bigger feet
than mine. I checked that this morning, before I gave her
the day off."

It hadn't taken Charlie too long to pull up my sheep
hook from the well, but he'd worked long and hard to
make sure there was nothing else down there. Whatever
else had helped dispatch Lloyd wasn't to be found.

"How would Gwen know about the old well?" Jilly
asked. "Even Charlie hadn't noticed it before, and he's
been all over the farm countless times."

"I don't know. As for Nadine, it seems unlikely she'd
be traipsing out in my fields looking for an old well to
hide a sheep hook. Here I was so certain she was guilty.
It's possible she had an accomplice, I suppose. Like her
handsome yogi."

"You're going to check her feet today, right?"

"Like Prince Charming searching for a murderous
Cinderella. We're looking for a size nine in a sensible
boot."

Jilly's inner antennae suddenly triggered. "What did Kellan have to say about all this?"

"Not much," I said. "Yet. I'm sure he'll send the hook to the lab, but I imagine the water will have destroyed anything useful."

Her green eyes bored into me. "You didn't talk to him, did you?"

"I left him a voicemail. He wasn't in when I dropped off the evidence."

"Ivy!"

"I just didn't want another lecture so soon after the last. I looped him in like I promised. Don't I deserve a nice, quiet funeral today? My nerves are shot."

She pursed her lips and looked around. "It looks like it will be quiet, all right. There's hardly anyone here. I figured people would be curious."

"Me too. When I was a kid, no one would miss a funeral unless they were violently ill. It's a social occasion in a small town. Plus... free sandwiches."

Jilly laughed and the funeral director, who was standing solemnly beside the guest book on its oak pedestal, glowered at us.

I gave him an apologetic smile and led Jilly over to sign the book. My arm was outstretched when a perfectly manicured hand landed on my sleeve.

"Nadine," I said, summoning a sympathetic smile. "How are you holding up?"

Her eyes were narrow and her lips formed a thin line. She was wearing a simple black wool dress, which set off the white glass pendant hanging on a fine silver chain.

My eyes widened at the sight of the necklace and she tipped her head.

"Surprised, Ivy?" she said. "I understand you're behind Chief Harper's recent visit. His fourth, I might add, each time with some new questions that seem to have emerged from your nosiness and speculation."

"Now, now," Jilly said. "What a tough day this is, Nadine. It's no wonder you're upset."

Nadine turned her dark gaze on Jilly. "You're no better than she is. I heard you flirted with Hayden. All he could talk about was your amazing flexibility. Best crow pose he's ever seen, he said."

"My mom got me into yoga young, that's all," Jilly said. "Decades of practice."

Nadine brought two fingers up so that I'd meet her eyes. "What are you looking at?"

"Your shoes," I said. "I'm sorry, I know it's the wrong time, but that's a gorgeous pair of alligator pumps."

"Reptiles are good for something," she said. "Now, let's talk about how Chief Harper came to doubt the security footage. He's seized Hayden's laptop." Her eyes darted wildly around the room as if looking for an escape. "There's private information on there."

"Even if you and Hayden have been a thing for a long time—since before your breakup with Lloyd, for example—you'd inherit everything, right?"

"What's left of it," she said. "He stalled and stalled, and I let him because I felt so guilty." Her eyes dropped to the somber charcoal carpet, about the color of my suit. "Now I'll look like the bad guy when we were on the rocks long before I met Hayden."

"That's all you need to say if word ever gets out. Which it won't from us, or Chief Harper, certainly."

"I loved Lloyd once, you know," she said. "We had a good couple of years before he took the dogcatcher job. That's when things went downhill."

"Don't be so hard on yourself," I said. "He was moving on, too, I think."

Her eyes sharpened. "He was? With whom?"

"It's all a blur now," I said, as Jilly pulled me away. "So much has happened since then."

We sat on the uncomfortable chairs in the last row. They were clearly designed to keep people upright and aware of the significance of the occasion. Over the next 15 minutes, a few familiar faces filed in: Gwen Quinn, Brian Letsky, the Scorpion and a dozen more I didn't recognize. It still left plenty of empty seats.

Just as the funeral director moved to the front of the room, Asher arrived and slipped into our row to sit beside Jilly. There was a little frisson of energy and I realized with a start that the interest wasn't one-sided. I stared at the back of Jilly's head as she turned to my brother. Could two highly distractible people focus long enough to get something off the ground? The thought of it made me anxious. I loved them dearly, and if things went south, one or both of them would be unhappy. But I'd never stand in their way.

I pushed the thought aside and spent the next few minutes studying the small group as best I could from behind. Brian and the Scorpion sat on opposite sides of the room looking equally subdued. Neither showed signs of guilt or discomfort, however. In fact, both pulled out their phones to play games while they waited for the service to begin.

Gwen sat alone. She'd given me a curt nod of greeting when she came in and then turned away. Although I'd only given her the day off, when she saw Charlie's truck roll in she must have figured her days as farmhand were numbered. She was right, too. It made my stomach clench to think of her clocking in for duty at the farm and then using her shift to find a good place to stash the murder weapon. Maybe she'd dug the hole first and then found the well. But unless Kellan had more to go on, there was no way to tie her to the crime other than a footprint.

I barely heard a word of the service, which was mercifully short. My mind was spinning with questions. Could a woman have strangled Lloyd without help? Or was there a man involved? There was no question a woman had been near the well, likely to dump evidence, but that didn't mean she was working alone. It seemed unlikely that Nadine could have found the old well, but Gwen had time and opportunity, with me being gone so much. She may even have moved it out of the hole to the cleansing waters of the old well.

Jilly must have noticed me shifting uncomfortably, because she patted my leg and whispered, "Calm down, Ivy. The way you're squirming, you look guilty. Or at least worried about Daisy looking guilty." She tipped her head and I saw my sister had crept into the back row on the other side of the room.

I gave Daisy a little smile, proud of her for showing up. It must have been difficult, even though Nadine probably had no idea about her tryst with Lloyd, and the twins.

When the service ended, I left Jilly and Asher with Daisy and went into the reception area. As expected, the few guests had descended on the refreshments like vultures. Brian and the Scorpion were plowing through sandwiches like woodchippers and didn't even notice me. My suit clearly retained some of its magical powers of disguise.

What I *hadn't* expected was to see Mandy McCain setting out refreshments. Her face was drawn and pale, but she was stoic as she arranged sandwiches. No one noticed she was setting them up in undulating coils like a python, because they were consumed almost before she set them down.

"Mandy, what a lovely tribute to Lloyd," I said.

Her eyes cleared a little as she recognized me. "Nadine hired me to cater. Wouldn't take no for an answer."

I led her to the quiet end of the table—the one with the trays of vegetables. "I mean the snake pattern. It shows you really cared about Lloyd and his interests."

A flush burned instantly in Mandy's cheeks. "You know about the snakes?"

I nodded. "Terrifying collection, at least to me." I smiled at her. "I guess you two were a little more serious than you let on."

"We weren't serious," Mandy hissed. "I couldn't get serious about a man who keeps dangerous snakes in a secret room, Ivy."

"But you liked him," I said. "That's obvious."

She moved celery sticks around on trays that hadn't been touched. "I admit it was nice to have someone care about me. You know how I am. I've had social anxiety since I was a kid and I've never dated anyone seriously. Lloyd courted me in the old-fashioned way, and he never pressured me. For half a second I got my hopes up that there was a happy ending for me." She gave a bitter laugh. "But there were snakes in paradise."

"Did you tell him how you felt about them?"

"He loved them. I couldn't ask him to give them up." She looked around the room. "In the end I was grateful for them. Being with him would have caused trouble and I don't handle stress very well."

"I'm sorry. Today must be hard."

"I'll be fine when this is done." She sighed. "It's just hard to imagine I'll ever meet anyone else in Clover Grove. You're always under the microscope here. You'll see."

"Oh, I already know that. And I'm single too, remember. But the game's far from over for either of us."

Mandy peered over my shoulder. "For you, the game's just beginning I think."

I turned and saw Kellan Harper standing in the doorway. My heart started racing, and not in a good way.

"Kellan and I haven't been a thing since high school. We had a terrible breakup. The kind you don't get over easily."

"Lloyd and I ended on a bad note, too," she admitted. She started moving the vegetables into the shape of snake coils, too. "Can you believe he gave me exactly the same pendant as he gave Nadine? I thought it was one of a kind. I felt special."

"You are special. A man like Lloyd doesn't define that. Where's the pendant now?"

"I gave it back to him. After I saw it on Nadine I hated it." She looked down and shook her head. "I feel bad now. I was so mad I snapped the chain and threw it at him."

"We all lose it sometimes," I said. "I certainly have."

Her eyes lit on Lloyd's widow. "She has no idea, of course."

"Don't feel guilty about liking Lloyd," I said. "Nadine had moved on, too, from what I heard. Who knows... maybe giving you the same necklace was his way of saying you meant as much to him as she once did."

"If that were true, he'd have finalized his divorce. How could I take him seriously when he just dragged things out?"

"When did you tell him all this?" I asked.

She picked up a tray. "Just hours before he died. When you told me about what he'd said that day about selling the store, I realized it would never work between us. Obviously I couldn't do that to my family legacy. So that was the last straw."

"How'd he handle it?" I spoke quickly, because Kellan was pushing through the sandwich crowd to join us.

"He didn't take me seriously at all. Like most people." She shook her head. "I expected more of a fight."

"I'm sure he would have fought for you later. If he'd had more time."

"It doesn't matter. Like I say, we weren't right for each other. Now, if you don't mind, I need to circulate. Some of the seniors can't make it to the table and need to be served."

She dropped a stack of napkins on the floor and I bent over to retrieve them. That's when I noticed her boots. They were a solid size nine, just a little bigger than mine.

CHAPTER TWENTY-TWO

K eats and I had tried a lot of activities in the two months I was recovering from my concussion. At first we focused on obedience classes, but they turned out to be a waste of time. Keats was naturally obedient and all I had to do was use a word once or twice and the command was locked into his brain. One trainer suggested we try activities to strengthen our bond, so we experimented with agility, flyball and even bite work. Most were entertaining enough, but our bond didn't really need to be strengthened. It had formed instantly the second his wet nose touched my hand for the first time and stayed 11 out of 10.

Keats was neutral about most of the activities, but herding he definitely liked. I guess it spoke to him on a primal level. In addition to sheep I tried him on cows and goats, but his secret passion was ducks. That's probably why he'd taken such a shine to Edna Evans' hens when they were loose. Even as a novice herder, he liked a challenge.

We'd been to several herding events outside the city before moving to Clover Grove. Now there was plenty of opportunity within an easy drive, but I didn't have time. Besides, Keats had plenty to distract him as my constant companion on the farm and in town. Even with his boundless supply of energy, he was tired at the end of the day, which was more than could be said of many young border collies.

Still, his ears pricked up and his nose worked over-time when we arrived at the Clover Grove sheepdog trial the day after Lloyd's celebration of life. Inside a huge fenced area were many smaller pens containing sheep, cows and goats. The crowd was larger than I had expected, but if there was one thing I'd learned since coming home it was that people liked an event—any event, it seemed. They might not be interested in herding but they were definitely interested in other people.

Jilly had forced herself to dress down for the occasion in capris, a T-shirt and sneakers. I wanted us to blend into the crowd, which was a little easier with so many herding dogs in attendance, many of them similar to Keats. We'd come in mid-afternoon when the throngs were at their thickest and the competition was heating up.

"Why do border collies have tails and Australian shepherds and corgis have none?" Jilly asked.

"It depends on their special expertise," I said. "Aussies tend to work in close confines, where their tails could be injured, so they get docked. Border collies work best in wide open meadows, so they get to keep their tails."

"I'm glad Keats has his tail," she said, smiling down at him. "It's his finest feature, other than the eerie blue eye that sees right through me."

Keats wagged his plumy white tip at her, proving he liked what he saw, inside and out. He hadn't warmed overly to anyone in Clover Grove, but Jilly got a free pass from our early adventures.

"I think I've lost my taste for herding as a sport," I said. "At one event a cow jumped a couple of fences when a novice was working with her. That made the cow unfit for herding and the farm shipped her to greener pastures. Of the heavenly variety. The woman whose dog caused the cow to run sat down in the paddock and cried. I worry about making the same mistake, so I'll probably only use Keats for real farm work, now."

"Okay. Wow. Then why am I here, in sneakers no less?"

I grinned at her. "Looking for clues. What else? Although I haven't ruled out Nadine, Kellan has. So now my forerunners are Gwen Quinn and Mandy McCain."

"Gwen I can believe," Jilly said. "But Mandy? No way. She's barely aggressive enough to beat egg whites."

We stopped to watch a woman running hard with her collie as the dog guided sheep around obstacles quite elegantly. It was like the two shared one mind. She barely needed the hook in her hand, but the sight of it sent a shiver up my spine.

"Is Keats going to show us his stuff?" someone asked.

We turned to find Gwen standing in the middle of a

group of gray-haired women, all wearing Clover Grove Herding Club caps with the black sheep on the crest. I recognized a few of them, including Myrtle McCain, who gave me a warm smile, and Edna Evans, who didn't. Gwen had a sullen air, no doubt because I'd officially laid her off with three weeks' pay, which was fairly generous, especially by Clover Grove standards.

"Not today, I'm afraid," I said. "We can't stay long."

"But you've said he's a natural, and we're all curious."

She crossed her arms and adjusted the brim of her cap. I was tempted to take up her challenge. Very tempted. But something felt off and I didn't trust Gwen not to set me up. Or worse, set Keats up. Dogs frequently got kicked, squished and stomped by angry horns and hooves at herding trials. I wasn't willing to take that risk just for fun anymore. Keats would have to settle for escorting his own critters around. When the animals all knew each other, it grew into a partnership.

"He is a natural," I said, looking down at my dog. His enthusiasm from earlier had disappeared and his tail was down. "With ducks, anyway. And I don't hear any quacking today."

"I guess that's why you didn't bring your hook," Gwen said.

My eyes darted up to meet hers. It was such a blatant taunt that it shocked me. She had no reason to know the missing hook had been found, let alone associated with Lloyd's death. Was she trying to make me look guilty again?

I started to speak but a sharp elbow in the ribs stopped me. "We need to mingle," Jilly told them with a bright smile. "With the inn opening soon, it's all business all the time."

"True," I said. "Is Mandy here, Myrtle?"

She shook her head. "Left her holding the fort. She's got so much business these days I can barely get her to cover for me. But today I insisted."

"Grandma needs a break, too," Edna said. "To hang out with her oldest friends."

"Agreed," Myrtle said, herding her friends away with a few swishes of her hook. "Let's catch Hazel and Beans with the goats in the next pasture. I can't believe how fast that girl can run at seventy-three."

"Closer to eighty," Edna said. "And she'll probably take the win again today."

After they left, Jilly turned. "That was odd. Gwen was a little aggressive. Do you think she guessed that the hook's been found?"

"Maybe she went back in the fields and saw we'd been working on the well. I guess we'll see if the shoe fits. Kellan is sending someone over to take a cast. I could see her foot was about right but it's clearly a common size." We walked back to the parking area, and I continued. "I feel like we may be getting closer to finding the killer, but I'm still leaning toward postponing the opening, Jilly."

"I know. I was just putting on a good front for the Herding Harpies." She patted my back. "When all this is over, guests are going to flock to Runaway Farm like ducks to a pond."

I managed a smile. "I haven't told the Flordale team yet, and I feel terrible. They have no place to go for their teambuilding retreat."

"Oh please. They were just being nosy and wanted to check out what you're doing. With their budget any hotel on the outskirts will take them at a second's notice."

I let Keats into the truck and climbed in after him. "It's probably for the best. I was desperate to show I was doing just fine after what happened. But I don't need to prove anything to them."

"You most certainly don't. They are so far in your rear view now, my friend."

That made me glance in my rear view, where I found the Herding Harpies standing like a row of gray-haired crows, watching me go.

Don't stall, don't stall, don't stall… I chanted silently.

I stalled the truck immediately, throwing Jilly into the dash once again.

"Sorry, you guys. The Herding Harpies psyched me out."

We both turned and saw the ladies leaning on their sheep hooks, or each other, laughing so hard I thought they might keel over.

"I guess that's exactly the reaction they're after," Jilly said. "Psyching you out."

"But why? Do they want me to fail here?" I gritted my teeth as I focussed on my driving. "I don't get it."

"Who knows? The small towns in Hallmark movies are sweet as can be."

"Clover Grove has always had a darker side." Once we were on the highway, the truck decided to cooperate. "People talked smack about us even when we were kids. My mom's a character and we were always struggling to get by."

Jilly pushed off the dashboard and sat back. "Which is why they're even more jealous that you walked into this arrangement with Hannah Pemberton, I suppose."

"Well, she'd met them all and chose me instead," I said, as we headed for town. "Is that my fault?"

"It's not your fault, it's your fate. But that doesn't mean people are going to be happy about it. The sooner you accept that, the more successful you'll be."

"Sometimes I wish I had my old grim reaper persona back. No one would mess with me then."

"That's not who you wanted to be anymore, remember? It's not who you ever were, and look at the toll that role took on you."

Jilly's head swivelled as we entered Clover Grove, and I sensed her credit card was looking for action.

"Starting the inn is taking a toll, too," I said. "What happens if the whole thing goes bust?"

She gestured for me to pull over. "It won't."

"It might."

"It won't." Her voice was insistent. "But if it did... you know I'd find you a new job in five seconds. You could make some coin, lick your wounds, and build from there."

"You make it sound so doable."

"Because I believe in you." She opened the passenger door and jumped out. "And I believe in Kellan Harper, too." She shut the door before I could answer and called through the glass, "I'll cab it back to the farm."

Her step was light as she headed for the only decent décor shop in town. Daisy had basically stepped down from her role since Jilly arrived, but that had more to do with keeping a low profile than disinterest. I had worried my two design queens would come to blows. But Jilly had embraced the country kitsch style Daisy had started and now they could both feel good about their contributions.

"I'm lucky, Keats," I said, as he rested his muzzle on my shoulder. "I know that sounds strange, given what's going on, but I thank whatever gods there be every day for you and Jilly and my family." He added his two cents worth with a low mumble. "Okay, and Kellan, too, I suppose. He is just trying to keep us safe. But it'll be a long time before I forgive him for threatening to seize you."

Keats gave an odd little peep that made me turn my head. There, on a side street just off the main drag, sat the world's smallest library. I hadn't been inside it, or even thought about it, since high school. On a whim, I turned the corner and then did a U-turn to pull up out front.

An elderly woman shook her cane at us from the front desk as we walked in. "You can't bring that mutt in here, Ivy Galloway. This is a library, not a dog park."

"Mrs. Bridges, how nice to see you." I walked right over to the desk. "You haven't changed a bit."

She shook her cane again. "Do not try to sweet-talk me. Not after that terrifying turn you made outside. Someone should report you to the township, and it might just be me."

"You're right, it was a bit reckless," I said, giving her my best down-home smile. Dottie Bridges had always been a tough nut to crack. "I just got a sudden urge to take a walk down memory lane. You know how many hours I spent in here as a kid. I borrowed piles of books."

"Unlike your siblings," she said. "You're the only one

who had any hope of—" She caught herself. "And yet here you are back, and with a hairy beast in tow. People have allergies, you know."

I made a show of looking around. "For the moment, we're the only two here. How about I agree to leave with Keats the second someone so much as sniffles?"

"Keats?" Her eyes narrowed. "What a terrible insult to one of the great poets."

Pointing to the stacks, I said, "I discovered the original Keats right there. You're the one who introduced me to the classics, and that's how I got a scholarship to college." I perched on the edge of the desk. "I guess I owe it all to you."

It looked like the pill would go down in the jam but then she collected herself. "You gave up your successful career to run a silly hobby farm. I won't take credit for that." She poked me hard in the hip with her cane. "Now get off my desk and take that mutt out of here."

I moved out of reach. "He's my therapy dog, Mrs. Bridges."

I rarely said that aloud but it was true nonetheless.

Mrs. Bridges finally settled her wings and lowered her cane. "Well, I was sorry to hear about what happened to you, Ivy, but I'm not sure I buy the therapy dog story. A border collie is more likely to *cause* stress than take it away. I've owned a few in my time."

"Not Keats," I said, stroking his soft ears. "He has the soul of a poet."

Pushing her glasses in place, she looked down at the index cards on her desk. "Fine. Go do what you need to do while the place is empty. We close in just over an hour."

"I'd like to look at back copies of the Clover Grove Tattler," I said. "I'm writing up some promotional material about the farm for my guests. I'm sure it was mentioned now and then."

"Whatever you like," she said, shuffling her cards.

"And the back copies are...?"

"Oh, Ivy." She gave me an exasperated look. "Everything is digitized now, even in this backwater town. I just keep my cards as backup in case it all comes crashing down. You're welcome to use our computer."

Laughing, I headed over to one of the three workstations and began searching for every reference to Runaway Farm, and its former names, in the paper and the town archives. There were more references than I expected and it was hard to tear myself away. It was harder still to believe the place was truly mine. What a gift.

Finally I got up and ambled to the door with Keats.

Mrs. Bridges watched me over her glasses. "Find what you were looking for?"

I shook my head. "It was a nice trip through the County's past though. Thank you."

It wasn't till I was turning into the lane at Runaway Farm that I pressed the brakes hard in sudden realization.

"I should have erased my browser history, Keats," I said. "Because I think I finally know who murdered Lloyd, and I hope Mrs. Bridges doesn't get to them first."

CHAPTER TWENTY-THREE

I left the truck parked haphazardly in front of the house and ran inside to change. There was one place I'd never thought to look for evidence and I wasn't going to do it in my street clothes. Squirming into my grubbiest overalls, I grabbed rubber gloves from the kitchen.

"Good thing there's a mask in the barn, buddy, because this could be gross. And I'm sorry to say I need your help."

Keats whined as he followed me down the path to the barn, as if to protest that there were no masks for border collies.

Charlie was still working short days as he recovered, so I didn't need to offer any explanations as I grabbed the only tattered mask I could see and went outside to climb onto the small tractor. It was one of my first investments, since the big old red tractor outside terrified me. I'd heard the stories of Hannah Pemberton riding around on it, but I was okay with letting her take the win.

Keats loped along beside me through the fields. Normally his tongue would be lolling in excitement, but today he looked tense, like a dog on a mission.

We drove out past the well, covered securely now that the investigation was complete. Then we passed the oldest orchard, where many of the apple trees were loaded with small, wormy fruit that kept the wildlife fat and cheerful.

After that, the brush gradually thickened but I could see deep grooves in the long grass and kept going. Finally the overgrowth was so heavy that I had no choice but to park. Getting off the tractor, I collected the gear I'd stowed in the carrier and started walking. The deeper tracks continued for a while. Bushes to either side were crushed and branches broken.

Someone wasn't afraid of the big tractor.

Keats found it first, of course: the old dump site. Technically, it wasn't on this farm's property anymore. It was part of land that had been severed and sold to a neighbor two decades ago.

Even from a distance I could see generations of garbage that included car parts, bicycles and even an old stove. A curious mixture of scents collided in the air: rust and moss and rotting wood.

We were searching for something fresher and more pungent. Keats quickly went into a point near two strategically arranged wooden doors. I walked around and looked down to find a large pile of manure. It looked to be at least a week's worth, and my menagerie produced a lot of it. Someone had gone to the trouble of carting a large amount of manure out here, moving it over the last long stretch by hand.

"Bingo," I said. "Unless I'm much mistaken, this is where we'll find our evidence. Good thing I brought the spade or we'd be here all night."

Keats offered up a stream-of-consciousness mumble that was quite intelligible to me. The longer we were together, the better I understood him. A few more months and I'd probably start mumbling and barking and whining back.

Today, English would have to do. "Keep your ears peeled, buddy. Out here, no one will hear me scream."

He panted anxiously, circling my legs and trying to herd me away.

"Sorry, no. But I'll be as quick as I can."

Slipping the mask over my face, I started scraping away manure, layer after layer, like an archaeological excavation. If I were a killer, I'd want at least a week's worth of crap on top of the evidence—enough to deter most amateur sleuths. I was invested enough to dig to the very bottom and pick each dropping apart if I had to.

In the top layers, I could easily recognize the deposits of the various livestock—cows, goats, sheep, alpaca and so forth. But underneath, decay blended them into one big, putrid mess. The warm weather we'd enjoyed had sped decomposition.

"I wish you could help," I muttered to Keats through the mask. "But I think your sharp nose would overload. This one's on me."

Mostly I was doing okay with the mask and mouth breathing, but when I spoke the stench crept in.

"Pardon me if I stop talking for a bit. I just... can't... breathe."

Keats kept watch, mostly repeating a semicircle. Every once in a while he'd go out and cover the whole dump area.

The deeper I dug the more despairing I got. What if I was wrong?

I couldn't be wrong. Once I saw the photo in the Clover Grove Tattler, I knew exactly what had happened. Well, I knew exactly *who* had happened and how they'd covered it up. Literally. Few people in this town would know the terrain well enough to find this old dump. There was no reason whatsoever for fresh manure here unless it was to conceal something.

Finally I shoved down the mask to pull in a long breath of so-called fresh air. Instantly I was enveloped in a toxic cloud that made me lightheaded. Leaning on the shovel, I bent over and hurled what was left of my lunch.

"I'm okay," I told Keats, who was circling my legs again in the hopes of herding me out. "Another half hour and I'll be through it."

He looked up at me and it seemed like there was a mixture of sympathy and disgust in his eyes. Stepping carefully past me on white paws that turned greenish-brown in the liquefying goo, he picked a spot and started digging.

"Thank you, buddy. I owe you one. I owe you a whole life of fun for this."

Snapping the mask back in place, I started digging again. After a while, everything seemed to swim in front of my eyes, and then suddenly, all went dark.

The sky was turning pink overhead when I opened my eyes again. I had no idea what time it was, but the days were so much shorter now. Fall really was coming in.

My mask was gone and I knew from the crusty feeling on my cheeks and forehead that I'd hit the muck face-down and either turned from my own primal urge to survive, or with a little help from Keats. Probably both. Charlie had warned me about the gases rotting manure threw off. They could even cause combustion. But I didn't think they'd knock me right out.

Keats' face loomed over me now. He stood on my chest, blocking the sky and the fresh air. "Don't," I croaked. "Smothering."

My caked lids parted a little more and I noticed something dangling from his jaws: a rubber glove.

I sat up so suddenly that I knocked him aside. He almost fell but of course adjusted on the fly, like always.

"You did it! You found it! You're a genius."

There was a neat little pile he'd gathered during my brief time out: another rubber glove, a trowel, and a baseball cap in a sad state. Reaching out, I scraped away a bit of crud from the emblem on the front to reveal a little black sheep. "Clover Grove Herding Club," it said. Just like the caps I'd seen on the Herding Harpies earlier, not to mention sitting on the shelf behind Dottie Bridges' desk at the library.

That's when I noticed the real find: a dog catchpole. The loop at the end of the long handle was made of wire and tightened like a noose. Lloyd had probably used it countless times to subdue or even strangle aggressive dogs. The tables had been turned on him.

I gathered the smaller items and stuffed them into my overalls, then stuck the catchpole under my arm. Everything was so caked in compost that it would be a miracle if any DNA had survived to identify the killer. But it was better than nothing.

Keats continued to herd me relentlessly as I got to my feet and trudged through the bush to the tractor. Normally he used posture, movement and glances to move animals from one place to another, but now he gave up on subtlety and poked me repeatedly with his nose.

"Message received," I said, climbing wearily on board. "The sun's going down and we've gotta boot it."

Despite his persistence, I took a moment to text Kellan Harper. My right glove had fallen off, leaving my bare hand covered in goo, so I slipped my hand up my pant leg where the fabric was clean, and scraped off as much as I could. Then I tapped out a message with my index finger. For good measure, I sent him a photo of the goods.

"Hit it, Keats," I said, firing up the tractor. "Let's see if we can outrun our stank."

CHAPTER TWENTY-FOUR

I left the tractor behind the barn and circled to the front to see if Kellan had arrived. There was no sign of the squad car, and the house was dark. Obviously, Jilly was still enjoying the attractions of downtown Clover Grove.

"Let's see to the livestock," I told Keats. As tired as I was, I had work to do. Such was the life of the hobby farmer. Luckily most of the critters were so hungry they came willingly to bed at night. All I had to do was leave the gates ajar and Keats did the rest.

He rounded up the sheep first with restrained precision. They trotted briskly ahead of him into the barn and I followed, ready to close the door to their pen. He spun and went back for the goats. The cows would be last. We had a routine and I trusted him. What's more, the animals trusted him. They waited their turn, sending up eager baas, bleats and moos. The alpaca, llamas and donkeys made a loud clamor, too. They stayed out all night but they still got their evening treats, which made everyone excited. Only Wilma was silent in her pen. She came last and her gate was locked until we were good and ready for her. As much as she wanted her evening repast, she wanted her freedom more. Keats and I had learned her sly swine ways. Even when she was locked inside, he circled back a few times to confirm.

I flipped on the fluorescent lights to ready the pens and stalls. As I turned, a twinkle on the floor caught my eye. There was something small and bright almost buried under a small pile of hay in the corner. Leaning over, I saw the loop at the end of a silver chain. Pulling out the fragment with the tip of my rubber-gloved finger, I realized it looked like the one that had hung the white stone pendant around Nadine's neck. I tried to pick it up but the chain was too fine, especially with all the crusty goop on my glove.

I knelt to get a closer look and figure out how to collect it without sullying any evidence that might be hiding in its tiny links.

So intent was I on the task that I barely noticed the sound of hoofbeats.

And I didn't notice the footsteps at all.

Suddenly something circled my neck, tightened and jerked me backwards. I fell on my back and a boot came down on my face hard and shoved my head to one side, pinning my cheek to the dirty floor. Pain exploded in my head and I wondered if my nose was broken. I squirmed in an effort to relieve the pressure on my throat but my attacker pulled sideways, obviously familiar with the desperate moves of a trapped animal.

My hands were free, so I reached up and clutched at the loop circling my neck.

Wire. Likely from another dog catchpole.

"Let me go," I said, my voice raspy. "The police are coming."

"I doubt that. You've been set on running the show yourself. Why change now?"

I managed to get my fingers under the wire and relieve just enough pressure to grab a couple of breaths.

"I had to stop," I said. "The chief threatened to take Keats if I didn't stand down."

"Huh. Hit you right where you live. I didn't think Kellan had it in him. He's always been soft. Especially where you're concerned."

I tried to turn and look her in the eye but she kept a steady traction, pushing on my hip with her boot and pulling on the catchpole.

"I can't lose my dog. Please, Myrtle."

"You're going to lose a lot more than that," she said. "But don't worry. I'll take Keats when you're gone. I like border collies and he's a smart one."

Rage rose like a tsunami and washed out much of my fear. "You'll never get Keats."

"Like you'll be able to stop me," she said. "Anyway, you know I'd never hurt a dog, Ivy."

"But you'd kill Lloyd?"

"And you. Sure." She took her boot off my head, placed it on the small of my back and shoved till I rolled flat on my stomach. "People are dispensable."

"Where is Keats now?" I asked.

"I snagged him with the catchpole and tossed him in

with the llamas. The fence is high enough to hold him."
She gave the noose a little jerk. "I wish I'd discovered
these earlier. Very handy device."

Pulling up on the noose, she kept her boot on the
small of my back. I pried at the wire with my right hand
and she said, "Ivy, relax. You're making this harder for
yourself. I always feel a little bad when it's time to send a
critter to the slaughterhouse. But at least they don't know
any better. They accept their fate, whatever it is. And
your fate is to buy the farm today."

Somehow she managed to keep the noose tight while
sliding a loop of rope over my left hand. She pulled on it
and then knelt on my back and grabbed my other hand.
In a second I was trussed up like a downed sheep, but at
least the pressure came off my throat when she needed
both hands to tie the rope.

"Myrtle." I gasped, pulling in all the air I could
knowing it could be cut off again any second. "Stop,
please. I understand why you killed Lloyd. I don't blame
you one bit."

Getting off my back, she rolled me over. Finally I
could see her face, and she was almost unrecognizable.
Her once-genial expression had transformed with rage.
Her cheeks were almost puce, her blue eyes were mere
slits and her teeth were exposed in a grimace. A Clover
Grove Herding Club cap covered her gray hair and a red
bandana circled her neck. She lifted the catchpole again,
ready to choke me as needed.

One gray eyebrow rose, too, giving me permission to
speak. "You were saying?"

"I know Lloyd was courting Mandy. That he turned

her head a little. She's such a shy, sweet person that she almost fell for it, too."

"He took advantage of her. Just like he did with your sister, Daisy." Myrtle's boot came down on my midriff. "He told me about her. He told me about a lot of things when he was in your position."

"He didn't take advantage of Daisy. Not really," I said. "Daisy made a mistake on the rebound after her husband left. But she didn't blame Lloyd for anything."

"Even after he gave her those red-headed ruffians? Crabs would have been preferable."

In any other circumstance, I'd have laughed. "Eventually he figured it out about the boys and started pestering Daisy. That's why she confronted him the day you... met up with him."

"*Killed* him. No point pussy-footing around, Ivy. Out here we're practical when it's time for a pest to go. And it was Lloyd's time." She pursed her lips. "I didn't expect that earful from Daisy. I was waiting outside on the tractor to get the jump on him, and heard it all. It only convinced me more."

"But you were wrong," I said, as she dropped the catchpole and turned to truss up my feet, swiftly and tight.

"I wasn't wrong about Lloyd Boyce, trust me," she said. "He wanted to get my store. I overheard you telling Mandy."

"Yeah. I guess he was working Mandy over to get at it because he needed the money. He was in debt. He had expensive hobbies."

"Better off dead. And now he is." She forced rope

between the loops around my feet and then ran it up to my hands and tied them together. Giving it a yank, she pulled me over onto one side and started dragging me across the barn floor. My time for talk was nearly over.

"It's Mandy you were wrong about," I blurted. "You underestimated her. She liked the attention from Lloyd but she figured out his game even before you... attacked... him."

She gave a hollow laugh. "You thought you could just ride into Clover Grove on your high horse—or alpaca— and become one of us. Yet you can't even use the word 'kill.'"

"Okay. So you killed Lloyd. Because you thought he'd exploited Mandy to drive you out of the store you've run for fifty years. That your dad and his dad owned before you." She was dragging me across the open space toward the back door and I kept talking. "I get it. But I can't go to the slaughterhouse with you thinking Mandy actually fell for it. She broke up with Lloyd the day you killed him." She stopped pulling abruptly and turned to stare at me. "Okay, let's go country: the day you *murdered* Lloyd."

"Go on." She leaned over to adjust the noose on the catchpole. The handle had been banging along beside me while she pulled me by the rope.

"Look over at the spot where you jumped me. There's the chain from the pendant he gave Mandy. She broke it and threw it at him just hours before you lured him out here. She'd seen the same one on Nadine that day. Then I told her about what Lloyd said about selling the store. Whatever she'd felt before that, she realized right then and there what he was all about. She left the store and met up with him and ended it. I guess he had the broken pendant in his pocket. The stone fell out in my field when you dragged him off."

"I didn't get far enough before I heard you stall the truck down the lane," she said. "I had to drop Lloyd and get the tractor back before you missed it. I'd planned to get him out to the old dump and deal with him later."

"How'd you lure him here in the first place?"

"I told him Keats was abusing your sheep and I'd meet him here to help. He brought an extra catchpole, which worked out well. That's why Kellan didn't realize it was missing from Lloyd's truck." She gave the one around my neck a tug. "Easy enough to buy another online. I'll never be without one now. Snag and drag."

"Don't you see it was all for nothing?" I said. "It was already over with Mandy. She would never have betrayed you like that, Myrtle."

Her jaw worked and she looked away. For a few seconds, I thought she might change her mind. Give this up. But she turned back with a look of resignation.

"Thanks for that, Ivy. You were always a kind girl. Too soft, like most of your family. But you were good to Mandy and I appreciate that now."

"Then let me go, Myrtle."

"Can't do that. The horse has left the barn. You know too much and I'm not going to jail. Mandy's not ready to stand on her own just yet. Poor thing's even softer than you."

"I don't deserve this. Like you said, I've always been kind to Mandy. Gave her a job, even."

"Kind and stupid. You just had to keep poking

around. I gave you a little rope, but you kept on sniffing. You're always going to be like that, thinking you know better than everyone else. It's better to choke you off like a weed, while I can. We were all watching, you know."

"The good ladies of herding?"

She snorted. "I wouldn't call us ladies, exactly. But yeah. Gwen helped me distract you by releasing your pig and getting Charlie out of the way. She even disposed of the evidence, which you clearly uncovered today. Honestly, I've smelled some terrible things in my life, but you're the worst. Edna kept a good eye on your comings and goings for me. And Dottie Bridges from the library let me know about your sudden interest in history today."

"I found out that you dated John Overlea, who owned the property fifty years ago. That's how you knew about the old well, and the original dump."

"He was a good man and he'd be horrified to see the spectacle it became in Hannah Pemberton's time. That ridiculous online TV show. Mandy loved it." She grunted in disgust and started pulling again. "People nowadays are idiots."

"Myrtle, please! There's still time to make this right. Mandy will run the store and work with me here at the inn."

"Sorry, love. All I can do is promise to give Keats a good home when you're gone. I owe that to you."

"Won't happen," I said fiercely. "I'd die before—"

"Exactly. Now you're getting it." We were at the back door, near the old tractor. "You've got two choices, chatterbox. Do you want me to knock you out before I drag you to the dump or do you want to enjoy the ride for a bit before a rock does it for me?"

"I'll enjoy the ride," I said.

She shook her head and smiled. "You're braver than I thought."

"Believe it or not, I've been through worse."

"It ain't over yet."

"Wait, wait," I said. "Would you please cover my head with a sack? I don't want to see Keats as I go. It'll break my heart." I gave a weak smile. "I figure you owe me that."

Sighing, she left me and went back into the barn to find a sack. That gave Keats a chance to come out of the shadows where he'd been lurking for a few minutes. I used my eyes and head to signal what I needed from him and, as always, he understood without words.

Myrtle clomped back, grumbling, and knelt over me with a burlap sack. When she was in exactly the right position, I yelled, "Now."

I jerked my head up suddenly, hitting her as hard in the forehead as I could. Meanwhile Keats leapt off the top of the hay pile and landed on her back. He climbed to her shoulders, grabbed her by the ear and pulled, snarling. She swatted at him but was so stunned by my headbutt she was awkward and clumsy. Finally she tipped onto her back.

Keats wasn't big enough to hold her down, but he was fast enough to keep her guessing. He leapt from one side to the other, nipping and worrying her hands, her arms, her face, her head. She jerked around as if being swarmed by wasps.

I rolled as far away as I could, dragging the catchpole behind me.

Finally Myrtle sat up and brought her fisted hand back, yelling in rage and ready to deliver a hard blow.

"Keats, off!" I yelled. "Run!"

Another yell, far louder than either of ours, echoed through the barn.

CHAPTER TWENTY-FIVE

I congratulated myself for not fainting a second time in one day. Turned out I could handle being choked and trussed up better than the heat and stench of the old dump. Just the same, I was happy to rest for a while with my head in Jilly's lap.

"Lotus position," I said. "Good thing you do all that yoga."

"Yeah. Hayden's going to be seeing plenty of me. I need to stay fit to keep up with you, Ivy."

"Where's Keats?"

"Same place as last time you asked," she said.

I raised my head and saw him reclining full-length from my chest to my legs. It was like he'd spread himself as far as possible to make the overall load light. I appreciated it, because I already ached and it was going to get worse before it got better.

"You okay?" Jilly asked. "I'm assuming so since you can still joke."

"I'm good." I tried to sit up but she pressed me down. Keats crawled up a little to anchor me. "Where is she?"

"Outside with Kellan. I think he hoped to take her down himself but Keats had done the heavy lifting. Asher picked me up in town and we all got here in time to see Keats jump off the haystack like a superhero." She reached out and stroked Keats' ears. "You are something else. I'm so glad I saved you."

"You?" I said. "Pretty sure I took the hard knocks in that rescue."

"Yeah, but we'd never have found him in the first place if not for me. Remember? You were running like a chicken with your head cut off and— Oops, bad analogy. I had this strong intuition to yell, stop! And there you were, standing in front of Keats and the sunflowers. I'm not taking the credit, though, because it was divine intervention."

I nodded and the movement made my head pound. "It was. Full agreement there." I tried to coordinate my right hand to pat the dog but couldn't quite manage it. He rested his muzzle on my hand, instead. A couple of tears leaked out of my eyes and ran down my cheeks.

"She caught him with the noose and threw him in with the llamas. He managed to climb the fence."

"Actually, he dug under. Or so Asher said, before he left to find the cows."

"The cows are gone?"

"And the goats. But the boys in blue will find them."

I sighed. "I left the gates unlatched so that Keats could bring them in but Myrtle had other plans."

I tried to sit up again but she held me down. "Relax. It's going to be fine, now. The inn can open. The cloud has lifted."

"Edna Evans will be thrilled she gets to hear the news first from Asher when he shows up in her garden with a flashlight. She's one of them, you know. The Herding Harpies who covered for Myrtle."

"Kellan will get to the bottom of it. Just rest now. You and Keats made his job easy."

"Excuse me?" Kellan loomed over us. "That woman fought like a wolverine." He raised his arm to show us double red semicircles. "She bit me."

"Seriously?" I said, and sat up suddenly. Fireworks detonated behind my eyes and I almost fell back, but Jilly propped me up. Keats shifted to my lap, and curled up with his white-tipped tail wrapped neatly around him. "Is she tied up?"

"Handcuffed to the tractor," he said. "She's not going anywhere for a long time."

I held out my hands. "Help, please. I need to see it with my own eyes, Kellan."

"You should rest a little longer." He gestured to my nose and forehead, which were no doubt showing signs of my struggle. "You've been through a lot."

Keats unfurled his tail and got off my lap with a resigned mumble.

"Just follow Keats' lead," Jilly said. "He knows what Ivy's going to do before she does."

Kellan pulled me to my feet with Jilly pushing from behind. When I was upright, he supported me with one arm across my shoulder and looped under my other arm. I had to admit, it felt nice to lean on someone other than a 40-pound dog.

Lights flashed in the darkness out in front of the barn as we walked out the back door. I heard a woman's voice calling, "Grandma? Grandma!"

"Oh for pity's sake," Myrtle said as we joined her. "You didn't bring Mandy here."

"Grapevine," Kellan said. "Edna, probably."

"Send her away. I don't want to upset her."

"It's a little late for that," he said. "You murdered Lloyd Boyce and were about to do the same to Ivy."

"Doesn't make me a bad grandmother. I've always looked after her. That's what I was doing then, too."

"Except she'd already looked after herself," I said. "She doesn't need you to look after her anymore, Myrtle. You can rot in jail without worrying."

She gave me a baleful look. "So the little puppy can bite after all."

"Yeah, I can bite, Myrtle," I said. "Not literally like you, though. Kellan will need rabies shots."

"You bit the police chief?" The voice was soft, but incredulous. Mandy had come into the circle cast by half a dozen high-powered police lights. Officers had swarmed the place, including my brother. I guess my attempted murder got him an automatic reassignment from highway patrol.

Myrtle looked down, momentarily chastened. "I did it for you."

"You bit Chief Harper for me?" Mandy said.

"I did *everything* for you. You weren't built for life out here, Mandy. People took advantage of you. Like Lloyd. That sly snake-lover saw a sucker and went for it."

"I'm not a sucker," Mandy said, glancing at me. "At least, not anymore. I can take care of myself. And I guess I'm going to have to."

"Mandy. Honey. Please don't sell the store. It's been in the family for—"

"I would never sell the store, Grandma. You should have trusted me more. In fact, I'll expand it."

"I don't want to change a thing."

"You don't get a vote anymore," Mandy said, more crisply than I thought she could. "You gave that up when you lured Lloyd out here and choked him to death. All you had to do was talk to me and I'd have told you."

"All you had to do was tell me first," Myrtle said. "Then I'd never have needed to kill him."

Mandy walked over to her grandmother and stared her down with blue eyes that had once been mild. Now they were harder, colder. "Don't you put this on me. None of it. I couldn't tell you about Lloyd because you always disapproved of my dating. You kept me penned up like an orphaned lamb. So when a man actually got around you and pursued me, I enjoyed it for a minute. Is it any wonder? But this lamb had horse sense. All it took was one look at those illicit reptiles to know. When Ivy told me what he had in mind about the store, I got rid of him myself. Without choking him to death, mind you."

"Your grandmother had been poisoning him, too," Kellan said. "Every morning he stopped at the store for his oatmeal to go, which she'd spiked with rat poison.

She'd been at it for weeks, judging from the takeout containers in his trash and the truck. It was wearing him down."

"Easier to kill a sick animal," Myrtle said, shrugging.

"So you were after him even before you knew about the store," Mandy said.

"I knew about the snakes though. Tried poisoning them first by spiking the mouse food a little. Didn't work, though."

Mandy shook her head sadly. "I don't even know you anymore."

"I did this for you," Myrtle said. "Don't—don't..." Her voice cracked and tears flowed down her tanned, wrinkled face.

"I don't hate you, Grandma," Mandy said. "You murdered a man. You tried to murder Ivy. And you bit a cop. You've clearly lost your faculties. So no, I don't hate you." She turned and looked at Kellan. "I leave you to deal with this."

She came over to me and took both my hands. My left was still covered in a filthy rubber glove. "Thank you. You've been a good friend to me, Ivy. I'm sorry about what happened and I promise I'll do whatever I can to make this up to you."

"It's okay," I said. "Just bake for me. Rock the taste buds of all my guests."

She forced a small smile. "You got it."

I felt a nose poking my thigh and realized that my strength was waning. Mandy released my hands and I leaned heavily on Kellan.

In one sweep, he picked me up and carried me out of the barn and up the path to the house.

"I had her, you know," he said. "The poisoned oatmeal, the prints in Lloyd's truck. If you'd given me one more day..."

"I know. Impatience bit me in the butt again. Or in this case, grabbed me by the neck. Thank goodness you got there in time to spare me the bumpy ride out to the dump." I looked up at him. "Don't leave Myrtle with my livestock for long. She might hex them."

He tipped his head toward the driveway, where a flashlight bobbed along. Soon the two cows came into view with my brother jogging along behind. He was using a garden rake to herd them, swishing it from one side to the other.

"This is fun," he called out. "I'm starting to get the attraction, now, sis."

"Keats," I said wearily. "Help him with the cows. Then find the goats. They're probably in the new orchard eating apples." I leaned back in Kellan's arms. "Gas guaranteed for tomorrow."

"Goat gas," he said. "Sounds lovely. Maybe I'll give it a day before I come for your official statement."

"Nothing could be worse than how I smell now, right?"

He fought a smile and failed. "I've been mouth-breathing. Won't do either of us any good if I pass out."

"This is so romantic," Jilly said, coming up behind us. "Ivy promised me a lot of things when she asked me to visit." She stopped on the stairs to watch Asher chase the cows into the barn. "I never imagined how thrilling it would be. I can't tear myself away now."

I leaned my head back over Kellan's arm to look at her and groaned at the pain in my neck. "You're staying?" I asked.

"Of course. No way I'd leave you in paradise alone. Keats, Kellan and Asher are worthy protectors, but a gal needs her best friend."

"I don't have enough eyes to manage her alone, that's for sure," Kellan said. He lifted his knee to support me while he opened the door, and then carried me inside.

"Could you cook me something, Jilly?" I asked. "Fighting for my life left me famished."

"You got it. And a couple of ice packs, too."

I gently patted my face, where I could feel dried blood. "Do you think my nose is broken?"

"Nope. Yours will still be prettier than mine, my friend. But you do need a shower. Or three."

Kellan set me on my feet outside the bathroom. "You okay from here?"

I nodded. Looking up at him, my eyes filled. "Sorry, Kellan. For everything."

He shook his head. "Never mind that now. I'm sorry for scaring you about Keats. He's a remarkable dog."

"He is. When I look back, I realize he signaled a change in Myrtle right after the murder. He'd liked her before, but the next day he jammed himself under my feet to get away from her. And he never wagged for her again."

"Good judge of character," Kellan said. "Hers had corroded."

"Yeah, and sadly, you were right: people who love dogs *can* commit murder."

"I hate being right about that." He sighed, and then glanced at Jilly. "I'll be back up to collect the evidence later."

"Good," Jilly said. "Wait till you taste my basil chicken."

CHAPTER TWENTY-SIX

Exactly one week later, Jilly and I put the leaf in the oak table so that it could seat more people comfortably. We'd recruited the Hodgsons, Teri Mason and Mabel Halliday, along with Daisy and her family, Asher and Kellan. I'd even invited Mandy, but she declined, sending along a couple of delicious apple coffee cakes to kick off harvest season.

"Isn't this exciting?" Jilly said, as we peeked through the kitchen door and watched everyone taking their places for our trial run for dinner at Runaway Inn. "The table setting and decorations are perfect, and I'm quite sure dinner will be a home run."

"You've worked so hard that I know it will be," I said, backing away from the door. "But with all the chicken dishes you've tried, I don't enjoy morning egg collection anymore. I feel so guilty."

"Me too," she said, going back to the counter to sprinkle fresh basil onto the serving platter. "That's why I made a couple of vegetarian dishes as well. I have the feeling you and I, at least, will be eating a lot less meat."

"I used to laugh when the vegans at work refused to eat 'anything with a face.' Now that I personally know some farm faces, it's different."

I paced nervously across the tile floor until Jilly told me to go into the dining room and sit down. "These are your guests. You need to socialize."

"I'd rather help you out here," I said.

"That's why we've hired Joel for the grand opening. He'll serve and you'll circulate. Your job is to make sure each and every person feels special and welcome. It needs to be a magical experience for people to spread the word and keep coming back."

I looked down at Keats. "I didn't think about this part of it when I decided to open an inn. We're aiming for magical."

"It'll get easier," she said, herding me to the dining room like a human sheepdog. "Would you trade this for your old life in Boston?"

"Let me get back to you with my answer," I said, pushing through the door.

I took my seat at the head of the table. Facing me at the other end sat Kellan, which couldn't have been an accident because Jilly left nothing to chance. There were place cards, and hers sat right beside Asher's.

Kellan smiled at me and I smiled back, touching the red marks on my neck that hadn't faded much after a week. The bruising on my forehead and nose was now an attractive shade of yellow. It was the second time in just a few months that I'd survived a deadly adventure, after 10 years of a sedate corporate existence. I was ready to enjoy some of the serene country living Clover Grove's marketing materials promised.

I knew that tranquility probably wouldn't begin until my former colleagues had come and gone, however. Flordale Corporation had been rife with politics before I left. They'd probably spend their entire stay at Runaway Inn squabbling, scheming and backstabbing. Hopefully they'd all get out of here alive and leave me in peace.

My nephew, Beaton, gave me a cheeky wink and pulled a long strand of fettuccine right off the serving platter. Then he tipped his head back, dangled the strand into his mouth, dropped it with a flourish and swallowed.

"Stop that!" Daisy said, slapping his hand. "Were you raised by wolves?"

His twin, Reese, threw back his head and let out a howl he'd obviously practiced a lot.

Keats, sitting on my left, raised his muzzle and howled, too. It was an eerie sound, not unlike the coyotes roaming in packs in the hills.

The boys dissolved in raucous laughter and I stared down at Keats in dismay. "That is inappropriate behavior for the innkeeper's dog," I said. "Manners."

Keats mumbled something deep in his throat and Asher laughed. "Back talk from all the boys. I like to think they learned it from me."

Jilly took her seat beside me and whispered, "Got an answer for me yet?"

"Yeah," I said, grinning at her as we held hands to say grace. "Bye-bye big city. I'm glad to be home."

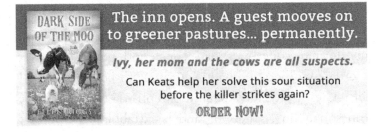
Please join my mailing list at *www.ellenriggs.com* for the latest news on the Bought-the-Farm Mystery series. I promise to share my pet photos and some other cool stuff.

Runaway Farm & Inn Recipes

Jilly's Chicken with
Dreamy Creamy Tomato Basil Sauce

Ingredients:

- 1 tbsp olive oil
- 1.5 lb chicken thighs (boneless, skinless and ideally organic)
- ½ tsp salt
- ¼ tsp pepper
- 8 oz tomato paste
- 2 garlic cloves, minced
- ¼ cup heavy cream
- 4-6 oz chicken broth
- 4 oz fresh spinach
- 8 leaves fresh basil (or ¼ tsp dried)

For serving:

- ¼ cup parmesan cheese, grated
- Optional: sautéed mushrooms.

Instructions:

Heat oil in a large frying pan on medium heat. Sprinkle chicken thighs with salt and pepper. Add them to the pan top side down. Cook for 5 minutes, until the top side is seared.

Flip the chicken thighs and sear for 5 more minutes on medium heat.

Remove the chicken from the pan to a plate. Drain the fat from the pan.

To the same, now empty frying pan, add tomato sauce, minced garlic, heavy cream and chicken stock. Bring to a boil and stir.

Reduce heat to low and add spinach and basil (plus sautéed mushrooms, if using). Stir until spinach wilts and reduces. Add more salt and pepper, to taste.

Add the cooked chicken back to the pan and increase heat to medium. Reheat the chicken thighs in the sauce until the chicken is completely cooked through and no longer pink in the center.

To serve, spoon the sauce over boneless chicken thighs and top with grated parmesan.

Delicious served over your favorite pasta or spiralized zucchini.

Mandy's Old-fashioned Apple Coffee Cake

Ingredients:

- 2 cups all-purpose flour
- 3 tsp baking powder
- 1 tsp salt
- 1/3 cup soft butter
- 1 cup sugar
- 1 egg
- 1 cup milk
- 1 cup grated, peeled apples
- ½ cup raisins
- 2 tsp cinnamon + 1/3 cup sugar for topping

Instructions:

Preheat oven to 350 degrees and butter a 9-inch square cake pan.

Mix dry ingredients with a fork.

Beat sugar and butter together with a mixer until light. With mixer on low, add egg and then milk. Stir in dry ingredients. Then stir in apples and raisins.

Spoon into pan and spread evenly. Combine sugar and cinnamon and sprinkle overtop.

Bake 35 minutes.

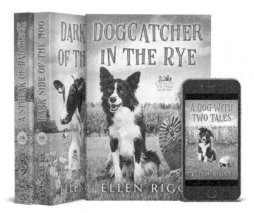

Made in the USA
Monee, IL
25 April 2020